THE
NONEXISTENCE
OF
RUTABAGAS
AND OTHER
MARGINAL
CONSIDERATIONS

JAN C. SNOW

WORTHPRINTING PUBLICATIONS   TWINSBURG, OHIO

Many of these pieces have previously appeared in the following publications:
*Akron Beacon Journal, Elyria Chronicle-Telegram, The Cleveland Edition,
Columbus Dispatch, Indianapolis Star, The Journal, New Cleveland Woman,
Norfolk-Virginian Pilot, The Plain Dealer, The Southbend Tribune,* and/or been
broadcast on WCLV-95.5 FM, Cleveland, Ohio, or WVIZ-TV 25, Cleveland,
Ohio in different form.

Worthprinting Ltd.
1791D Rolling Hills Dr.
Twinsburg, Ohio 44087

Library of Congress Catalogue Number 86-050115
ISBN 0-9609734-7-8   (paperbound)

Printed in the United States of
America

All the people who deserve
to have this book dedicated to
them know who they are.

jcs

CONTENTS

COMMENTS

Your Generic Critic Reviews Everyday Establishments, #1

SUGGESTIONS

Your Generic Critic Reviews Everyday Establishments, #2

ONCE AROUND THE CALENDAR

Your Generic Critic Reviews Everyday Establishments, #3

MOSTLY TRUE STORIES

COMMENTS

JUNK, STUFF, AND OTHER GARBAGE

We all know what garbage is. Garbage is that which we'd rather not swallow, be it foodstuffs or ideas. Occasionally it's merely a matter of age, in that a lot of garbage is food we would eat if only it were newer.

I'm not too fond of garbage, primarily because it smells bad. It's a subjective judgement on my part and I'm willing to admit that acceptability of bouquet may be in the nose of the beholder but, nevertheless, that's one of my reasons for not liking garbage. I do, however, really enjoy junk.

Almost everything starts out as a valuable. Some things remain valuables, but most quickly degenerate into things. If moderately useful and the correct size, a thing may remain a thing for an indefinite length of time. More likely, after a short while, it becomes part of your stuff.

Complete familiarity is necessary for a thing to become stuff. A silver tea set, for example, never becomes stuff, no matter how long you have it. For most people a silver tea set remains a valuable. If you have three or four of them, they probably become things, but a silver tea set is too formal ever to become stuff. Leave it on a shelf in the basement for eight years and it may turn into junk, but it will never be stuff.

As with grownups' possessions, everything a kid has starts out as a valuable. Whatever it is, it remains a valuable for about five days during which the kid will carry or wear it everywhere, sleep with it, take baths with it and introduce it to total strangers.

At the end of this time period, some magic secret signal goes off and the item ceases to be valuable. Overnight it becomes part of the kid's stuff, or it goes straight to being junk. Kids almost never have things.

Stuff becomes junk when it gets broken or doesn't fit, or when you just don't want it anymore. Some stuff becomes junk only when the closet gets full. A great deal of stuff and a lot of things become junk when you start packing to move to a new house.

Without the aid of the Federal government, an elaborate system for the communal exchange and equitable redistribution of junk has been developed in this country. These privately administered junk redistribution events are known as garage sales, yard sales, house sales, or in some areas, tag sales. What they really are, of course, is junk sales.

The true beauty of this system is its ability to transform junk into valuables, thereby beginning anew the sequence of ownership and recycling the nation's material goods for the benefit of all. No matter what kind of junk you're getting rid of, sooner or later someone will show up who recognizes your junk as a potential valuable and will pay money for it . . . which is another reason I prefer junk to garbage. Who would buy your garbage?

———————

STORM WARNING

NEWSFLASH . . .

Communities throughout northeast Ohio have begun the tremendous job of trying to recover from the onslaught of weather-related news reports that killed at least six local television news broadcasts last week and injured scores of others.

Dozens of minicams, remote van units and news choppers slashed through the area, leaving a path of destruction that extended across prime time in northeast Ohio and into western Pennsylvania and southern Ontario. On-the-spot news reporters were reported on the spot throughout the vicinity.

In Ohio the broadcasts began shortly after 5pm last Friday and continued unabated for four to five hours. Between "Merv Griffin" and "Miami Vice" more than 75 special reports, updates, interviews, alerts, watches and warnings struck in one hundred and ten different communities in seven counties.

State officials labeled it the worst broadcasting disaster since the snowstorms of last winter during which viewers were bludgeoned for nearly six straight weeks with euphemisms for precipitation. In Akron, at least two dozen television viewers smothered by updates required resuscitation and in Elyria entire blocks stayed tuned for further bulletins.

The govenor declared emergencies within four cable franchises, making them eligible for assistance from National Guard troops who are expected to move in early next week to begin issuing library cards.

The broadcasts that rampaged throughout northeast Ohio Friday were fickle and capricious, ravaging entire half hours of air time but skipping over others, boring and annoying randomly. In the small community of Madison-on-the-Lake, 113 families were gathered in front of their respective television sets to watch "Wheel of Fortune." A weather update came within mere seconds of interupting the bonus round.

Others in nearby Ashtabula weren't so lucky. Just as the contestant spun for the $17,000 automobile, their screens were obscured by crawlers warning of the possibility of the necessity to watch for a warning to watch for tornedo warnings or watches.

Such phenomena are difficult to control and one could strike again at any time. Meanwhile, experts recommend that you equip the southwest corner of your basement with the following emergency supplies: four quarts of water, one warm blanket per person, two boxes of peanut butter chocolate chip granola bars, and a Dorothy L. Sayers novel. And at the first sign of an extended weather story, for your own safety and that of your loved ones, unplug your television set.

LITEN UP

While the magic advertising words of a few years ago were "all natural" and "nothing artificial," today's marketing *abracadabra* is "light." Everything, it seems, is becoming lighter and lighter just as fast as the manufacturers can slap on the new package labels.

This new light is not the light that is the opposite of dark. This is light as opposed to heavy: light as in of relatively low weight, low density, having less quantity, intensity, length or volume than normal. Even the word "light" has lost weight, having slimmed down from five letters to four, in most cases.

You can buy lite mayonaise, lite salad dressing and lite cottage cheese. There's lite beer and lite wine, and to munch lightly (or litely) with your drink, lite corn chips. There are lite frozen shoestring potatoes and lite canned carrots, crispy lite crackers and lite cream cheese. Fast food places feature new lite menus which now make it possible to spend more money more quickly for fewer calories.

Light (or lite) is no longer limited to food. An international fashion conglomerate recently introduced a new light product which is described as a lighter-than-cologne scent for men. "A lightly scented yet bracing men's fragrance," it says, "designed for everyday use from morning until evening." Described as ideal for work or play, it can, the manufacturer promises, literally be splashed on without risk of over-applying. (You could, of course, achieve the same results by adding a great deal of water to your present cologne. As it is, if you want to wear your new light cologne on a heavy date, you'll just have to boil it down.)

As the trend to lite continues, we can look for additional non-food products to appear wearing the lite label. Although they're not yet designated as such, a number of this season's

17

new television programs have at least 43 percent less entertainment value than last year's shows, making them worthy of designation as lite programming.

Lite symphonies could be created from the old heavy classics by asking the strings to play only every other note and lopping off the ends of phrases so as to avoid harmonic resolutions. "Lite Mozart — now with 23 percent fewer cadences."

Look soon, too, for the new lite light, a lite light bulb that delivers 37 percent fewer lumens while using the same wattage as a heavy light bulb. The lite light eliminates harsh glare and actually makes you look thinner by shedding 17 percent less light on the subject.

More and more these days, more is less and less all the time . . . more or less.

NO MORE JANITORS
(and other bad news)

I am not looking for a job . . . really, I'm not. I have enough (more than enough) to do now. The only reason I started reading the classifieds was to find out what hairdressers are called these days.

My quest was occasioned by the re-reading of an essay by H. L. Mencken. Published in 1936, Mencken's discussion centers around the use of realtor for real estate agent, although his catalog of occupational euphemisms includes mortician, electragist and the Table-Waste Disposal Department of the City of Pasadena.

Hairdressers, Mr. Mencken found, had been replaced by beauticians, although it appeared that their functions remained the same. Only the name had been changed. (To protect the indigent?) Judging from my recent study of the classifieds, during the intervening half-century the beautician also has become an endangered species, yielding for the most part to the cosmetologist.

For one whose primary activity is the manipulation of tresses, cosmetologist would seem the more accurate term. Its roots (dark or otherwise) are in the Greek *kosmetos*, well-ordered, from *kosmain,* to arrange, which is derived from *kosmos*, meaning order. That all makes sense when considered in light of what most hairdressers try to accomplish. What doesn't make sense is encumbering the profession with a title aping that of an academician. What's wrong with hairdresser?

Cosmetologist certainly is easier to defend than some similar occupational titles: mixologist, for example, which implies a specialist in the principles of mixology, whatever that is. If bartender is somehow not a classy enough identification for these makers of alcoholic concoctions, why not simply mixer, as in, one who mixes?

Like -*ology* , the suffix -*ian* seems have been invested with dignifying properties and therefore, job titles formed with it tend to be held in higher esteem than those they replace. Auto technician is a fancy term for mechanic. A mortician is only an undertaker and, as previously noted, a beautician by any other name is still a hairdresser.

My recent excursion through the classifieds turned up an ad for a sanitarian, whose delineated duties sounded indistinguishable from those of a health inspector. Unlike mixologist, sanitarian is legitimized by the dictionary, but what's wrong with calling the person a health inspector?

Sanitarians or health inspectors, they probably find that buildings aren't as clean as they used to be. It's no wonder; there are no more janitors. There are only building superintendents and maintenance people. Upstairs in the office, administrative assistants have replaced the secretaries and there are word processing specialists where the typists used to be. No one's in the personnel office; they're all over in the human resources department. And sitting in the payroll office is a compensation administrator.

Schools no longer have janitors, either, though they are usually fortunate enough to have custodians. Where the librarian used to work, there's a media specialist. Truant officers have been replaced by visiting teachers and the coach is now the athletic director. Also in the general area of education, somebody out there is advertising for an electronic instructor. Surely what is sought is someone to instruct a class in electronics . . . not a robot that teaches.

Salespeople also have disappeared (which may explain why it takes so long to get waited on when you're trying to buy a raincoat). A person who sells things for a living is now a marketing representative, sales consultant, account representative, sales engineer, retail consultant, or occasionally, retail clerk. Beauty *counseillur*, one of my recent discoveries, ultimately translates into cosmetic salesperson, which brings us to another question: what's wrong with calling the stuff makeup?

Garbage collectors have, of course, become sanitary engineers. Camp counselor has metamorphosed into outdoor education intern and the head mechanic is now the vehicular maintenance director. Internal plantscapers are sought, with positions available for installers and maintenance technicians. What the prospective employers are trying to say is that they need some folks to carry in the plants, and some others to go back from time to time and water them!

Even in 1936, there weren't any press agents. They were all in public relations. Today, practitioners of public relations masquerade as various directors and managers of communications, external relations, press or media relations, and departments of community information and news services.

In the ever-mystical world of non-profit institutions, development means fundraising. So does institutional advancement, although that also may mean public relations, which in academic institutions may be dubbed college or university relations. Alumni relations (which sounds like your cousins who've graduated) inevitably doubles back to fundraising, too.

Smoking cessation instructor, though silly, at least is understandable. Aesthetician is not, although the context within which it appeared leads me to suspect cosmetic (read "makeup") sales again. The duties of a revenue reimbursement specialist were not explained either, but the ad did say she or he "will interface with various levels of management," presumably while they're trying to get their money back.

One ad, clear and simple, held particular appeal for me: "Cleaning trainee — no experience necesary." If ever I decide to stop writing and get an honest job, I may apply for that one. At least I'll know that I meet the qualifications.

THE GREAT AMERICAN PASTIME

An excerpt from my dissertation, *An In-Depth Examination of the Psychological Revelations of the Literary Symbolism Contained in the Lyrics of the First and Perhaps Only Verse of the Well-known American Folk Hymn, "Take Me Out to the Ball Game."*

Consider the opening line. Couched in the imperative this line reveals a demanding, infantile view of the world which sets the tone of the entire work. In refusing to confront the possibility that he might take himself to the ball game, the author reveals his feelings of inadequacy, and gives indication of his sexual impotence.

The second line extends the use of the infantile imperative established in the first line. The author's desire to be "with the crowd" shows us his extraordinary craving for acceptance. He not only desires to be "taken out" but has a compelling need to be "with the crowd," signalling his need for unconditional love and revealing his feelings of lack of self-worth.

At first glance, the third line, with its request for the purchase of sustenance, merely expresses feelings of economic dependence. Deeper meaning, however, can be found in the craving for non-nutritious foods, such as peanuts and crackerjack. The author's inability to control his consumption of these harmful substances shows his deep disturbance and is indicative of the low self-esteem typical of individuals who suffer from eating disorders.

The fourth line is a clear rejection of acceptance of responsibility. In admitting that he doesn't care if he ever gets back, the author reveals that his failure to develop more adult patterns of behavior is hampering his ability to form a stable sexual relationship due to his unreliability, and is in conflict with his partner's needs for security and predictability within the relationship.

All the mindless rooting for the home team which follows in the fifth line is an indication of narrow chauvinism, demonstrating a personality whose critical capacities are poorly developed. Such unquestioned loyalty to the home team based strictly on geographical proximity is but a milder manifestation of the fanatic behavior encouraged by totalitarianism and is incompatible with successful existence in a democratic society.

Studies of the childhood behavior of criminals reveal callous indifference to the feelings of others, such as that shown in the sixth line. Unwilling to deal with the consequences of identifying with the team members' difficulties, the author dismisses the possibility of their not winning as "a shame," thereby protecting himself from the emotional devastation he would experience were he to allow himself to respond empathetically to their plight.

The fascination with violence revealed in the seventh line tells us the author is hungry for human contact and physical closeness. Unable to develop a mature relationship, he takes refuge in violent behavior, "striking out" as a negative means of gaining the attention he needs. Most likely the author was himself a victim of violent abuse as a child, and without intervention this cycle of destructive behavior will continue with the next generation.

The final line completes the cyclic form of the poem by harkening back to the first line, but with an important difference. The adjectival use of the word "old" shows the author's nostalgic longing for a remembered past, a simpler time which perhaps never was, and when viewed through memory, was indeed a happier one for all of us, even if it never occured.

———————————

NONE OF THE ABOVE

I thought that when I finished school my days of test-taking would be over: no more quizzes, no more exams, no more questions to answer or blanks to fill in. Of course, I was wrong.

Not long ago I received a questionnaire in the mail from the International Olive Oil Council. "In order to be able to help in the most efficient way all those who are interested in learning about olive oil, we should like very much to have your kind help. We are enclosing a questionnaire and addressed envelope which we would be most grateful to receive from you."

Olive oil? I'm not Italian. I've never even been close to the Mediterranean. Tomato paste makes me break out and I can barely pronounce *linguine.* I don't know anything about olive oil. For fear of receiving a failing grade, I tossed the communication in the round file without reading the questions.

In the same mail a pamphlet from a local utility company urged me to take their home energy quiz. "Is the air conditioner really needed every time I use it?" "Is my insulation adequate?" (Mine certainly is, although I'm not sure I can say the same for the house.)

"Do I take showers instead of baths?" "Am I washing in cold water whenever possible?" That's a little personal. I don't think I want the people at the utility company to know whether or not I take a lot of cold showers.

From the bank there was *The Smart Consumer's Guide to Getting Loans.* "Could you get a loan today?" it inquired. "Take this test and see." No thanks. I'm a writer. I'm smart enough to know the answer to that one.

The magazines were even more demanding. "Are you a modern romantic, a cultured classic, an outdoor active or a sleek sophisticate? Take this quiz and find out what your beauty personality is." I took the quiz and found out I was none of the above. I don't have a beauty personality.

"How long will you live? Amazing medical quiz foretells your future." According to this test, I'm destined to live to be 86 plus. I'm not sure I can face that many more decades with no beauty personality.

"Rate your mate," another quiz commanded. "Find out how you work as a couple." A couple of what? "How do you score as a parent?" "What's your creativity quotient?" "Will you have an affair?" I scored in the second highest group on this one, indicating that I'm a poor risk in the fidelity department.

"What does your sleep position tell about you?" This was fun. There were a few questions, plus cute little diagrams of bodies arranged in an amazing variety of poses, some of which I think are impossible for a person of my age to assume without extensive training in gymnastics. I answered the questions and turned to the back of the magazine to score the results.

The results indicated that my sleep position shows I have a compulsion to regulate the events of my waking life. Well, what person doesn't? Especially if she has recently learned she's married the wrong person, isn't very creative, and has no beauty personality.

THE STEP-FAMILY GAME

Rapidly gaining in popularity, the Stepfamily Game is being played by ever-increasing numbers of Americans each year. All the rage in city, suburb and rural hamlet alike, this fascinating and fun-filled experience is now enjoyed by millions all across the United States.

I. Equipment

The Stepfamily Game is played on a life-sized board with loaded dice. Player tokens are described below. No other equipment is needed.

II. Preparing to play

There is nothing that will prepare you to play the Stepfamily Game.

III. Beginning the game

1. The Stepfamily Game begins when the participants share the same living space for any time period exceeding 72 hours.

2. Once begun, play may not be suspended.

3. Play continues uninterrupted seven days a week, including Sundays and holidays.

IV. Object of the game

Simple survival.

V. Players

1. Minimum number of players required is three — one adult of each sex and at least one child, any gender.

2. There is no maximum number of players, the limit being defined only by circumstances and the size of the living space in which the game is played.

3. Players include the Arbitrator, the Instigator, the Martyr, the Innocent Bystander , the Left-out and the Perpetually Perplexed Adult. Choose three or more,

depending on the number of participants.

NOTE: It is traditional to play the Stepfamily Game with at least one Other. An auxiliary player, the Other does not move around the board but maintains a position off to one side of the game and delivers a detailed commentary on the moves of the adult players. Although the Other has no token and does not directly participate in the game, this player's influence on the final outcome of the game should not be underestimated.

VI. Player tokens

1. The Arbitrator may be played by an older child or either of the adult players. This player's token is a tattered white flag large enough to hide behind.

2. The Innocent Bystander most often is played by the youngest child but may be played by any member of the family. Regardless of the player, the token used by the I.B-S is a wide-eyed look.

3. The Perpetually Perplexed Adult usually is the paternal player. His token is an open wallet.

4. The Left-out, frequently, but not always, played by the middle child, refuses all available tokens and complains throughout the game because he does not have one.

5. The Instigator is played by any of the children, and occasionally by one or both of the adults. Many families play the Stepfamily Game with more than one Instigator for added excitement. The Instigator's token is a book of matches with the cover left open.

6. The Martyr is always the maternal player. Her token is the largest on the board and consists of a pile of eighteen smaller tokens, each representing one duty or responsibility. Any other player who attempts to remove any part of the Martyr's token is subject to extreme penalty.

NOTE: All players, with the exception of the Martyr, may exchange tokens at any time.

VII. Method of play

1. All players proceed around the board in the same direction, except the P.P.A., who wanders about the center of the board changing directions with each move.

2. The number of squares advanced each move is determined by the throw of the dice.

3. Any time the child players receive unequal throws, both of the parent players are subject to penalty.

4. Regardless of the number showing on the dice, the Instigator may jump ahead and displace any other player's token.

5. The I.B-S may rethrow the dice as many times as she pleases until a satisfactory number is thrown. No other player is permitted to do this.

6. On his first move, the Left-out places himself in the penalty box and remains there for the duration of the game.

7. The Arbitrator may block any move of any other player.

8. Every fourth move of the Arbitrator must be spent trying to coax the Left-out from the penalty box.

9. The Martyr is required to advance around the board three times as rapidly as the other players.

VIII. Ending the game

Play continues until one adult or all children leave the living space.

IX. Winning the game

The Stepfamily Game is won when all players agree voluntarily to turn in their tokens. Potential Stepfamily Game players are cautioned that the statistical odds of this occurring have been calculated to be 18,973,429:1.

Yuppies, Muppies, and Moppies

BMWs, personal audio systems, 70 percent Brie, and running shoes that cost more than your first car. We all recognize these as the accouterments of those heroes and heroines of the new marketing age, the Yuppies.

The young urban professional, *Homo yupius*, is the marketers' darling. Earning by definition more than $30,000 a year, these conspicuously consuming baby boomers are characterized by a clear-eyed gaze which is unclouded by anything stronger than white wine and is firmly fixed on the horizon of success. Other identifying marks include a right hand permanently wrapped about the handle of a genuine leather attache case and a middle on which "you can't pinch an inch."

Marketers are overlooking a much more sizable segment of the population, the Yuffies. Earning $10,000 or less annually, these young urban failures, according to one marketing newsletter, outnumber the Yuppies among the baby boom population five to one. All Yuppies may be baby boomers, but not all baby boomers are Yuppies.

Worth remembering, too, is that not all adults are baby boomers. Some, on the leading edge, might better be described as Muppies (mature urban professionals). Directly above the Muppies, chronologically speaking, are the Moppies (mature older people).

Moppies and Puppies (poor urban persons) make up a larger portion of the population than marketers acknowledge and are not to be confused with Mommies (mainly optimistic middle-aged), Poppies (primarily overweight people) or the Mammas and the Poppas, a defunct singing group of Moppies that included one Poppie.

29

Statisticians tell us that the majority of the American population is made up of Guppies (grownup people) of one sort or another. Among the Guppies we find subgroups such as Floppies (fat, likable, older people), Flappies (fit, lithe, active people) and Mummies (mostly unattractive men). Of much less importance statistically are the Happies (hyperactive adolescent persons) and the Yappies (young adult Presbyterians).

New segments of the population such as Gummies (generally unfulfilled mothers) and Bummies (bearded Unitarian ministers) are being identified every day by the Mappies (marketing and advertising professionals).

Assuming that the marketers continue to segment their audience and accelerate their efforts at the current rate, it won't be long before all of us except the Mappies become Daccies (disgusted American consumers), who will respond by refusing to buy anything at all.

HAUTE COUTURE CUISINE

I t had to happen. First the American public covered its collective backside with monikered denim. Signature T-shirts were followed in rapid succession by designer ties, belts and even socks. Having exhausted the general category of clothing, the designer-products folks turned to pseudo-apparel such as watches, sunglasses, makeup and fragrance and then sold us designer luggage in which to carry it all.

Our bodies now completely covered with advertising, the designers covered our beds and baths as well. They sashayed into other areas of our homes with designer desk accessories and designer cookware. The harbinger of the next frontier to be conquered by standardized chic was designer chocolates. The emergence of designer food was inevitable.

Although designer food is not emblazoned with the initials of its perpetrators, it is easy to identify. Like most designer products, it tends to be somewhat overpriced and not particularly substantive. Designer food, by the way, is not to be confused with celebrity food such as Roy Rogers roast beef and Pearl Bailey chicken. That's altogether another matter.

Potato skins are designer food. Zucchini sticks are designer food. Cold pasta is definitely designer food, as is any dish which uses artichokes in an unnatural manner. Most chocolate cheesecake is designer food and so is coffee with cinnamon in it.

Any hamburger that weighs more than a quarter-pound and has its own name is designer food. Hamburgers topped with anything resembling chip dip are also designer food. Omelets with exotic additions such as asparagus or Gorgonzola cheese are designer food, and ratatouille clearly exhibits designer tendencies.

Often designer food is ethnic food wrenched from its proper context. For examples, nachos served anywhere the waiters do not speak Spanish are designer food. Ditto for most menu items containing avocado. Anything served in pita bread is designer food, unless you are eating in a Lebanese restaurant or a vegetarian lunchroom operated by the Disciples of Yoga.

The trendiness of the foodstuffs offered is usually signaled by other aspects of the dining establishment. For example, if the restaurant carries a name utterly unrelated to the serving of food, such as "The Plumbing Supply Company" or "The City Morgue," designer food is likely. If the building in which the restaurant is housed was originally a bank, waterfront warehouse, police station or municipal bus garage, designer food is inevitable.

Designer food is served in surroundings that are decorated in a style future historians of interior design will most certainly label *nouveau quiche*. Ferns are emblematic of designer food. Butcher block tables and/or formica tables made to look like butcher block tables are symptomatic. Walls and ceilings often are littered with old bicycle wheels, farming implements, fire hats and stuffed moose heads. Stained glass, Art Deco trappings, vintage movie memorabilia and old chuch pews are also indiciative of designer food. Tablecloths, on the other hand, are a sure sign of non-designer food, as are waiters wearing real ties.

Certain *modus operandi* also are identified with designer food. Tableside cooking is not designer food. Neither are dessert carts. Interminable listings of specials illegibly scrawled on a blackboard usually are designer food. Salad bars used to be designer food, but are no longer. Pasta buffets and Szechuan brunches are definitely designer food.

Designer food isn't necessarily bad. In fact, much of it is quite tasty. And while it isn't what you'd eat to get you through a hard winter, it does indeed supply some nutrients. A particularly rich source of craze, designer food also provides the adult minimum daily requirements of both mode and fad. Limited amounts of swank and swish may be present, along with traces of *dernier cri*.

Designer food is on nearly every street corner and in absolutely every mall. Because of its ubiquitousness, designer food is eaten by almost all of Western civilization from time to time. It has emerged as a dietary staple among persons whose warm-up suits have never experienced sweat. Most designer food, however, is consumed by ordinary, everyday citizens, Americans like ourselves, our relatives, friends and neighbors — we who lack designer bodies, because we'd rather eat designer food than look good in designer jeans.

———————

FINANCIAL PLANNING FOR THE OPTIMISTIC

I finally solved my investment problem. (In the past, my problem had been that I had no money to invest.) It only took about an hour and cost less than two dollars. What I did was enter all the sweepstakes offers that came with my Sunday newspaper.

The complete home entertainment center I could win includes a 46-inch screen rear projection television; a video cassette recorder and movie camera/recorder; stereo amplifier, tuner, turntable, tape deck, speaker system and headphones; 13-inch color television with remote control; and cordless telephone. According to the folks who are giving it away, this mass of electronic marvels is worth $100,000. I figure I could sell it all and, with careful planning, live on the proceeds for about five years, by which time I expect to have won something else.

There's a chance I'll want to keep the stereo components since my record player delivers monaural Haydn with all strings and no winds, but that still would leave enough cash for three to four years, depending on inflation. I'd also kind of like to keep the 13-inch color television, but I'm definitely getting rid of the 46-inch screen rear projection television. There's simply nowhere to put it in my living room.

Of course, I might also win the vacation home of my dreams, in which case I'd have room for the 46-inch screen rear projection television. And if I win the hot tub, I'm going to need the cordless phone, too. Now that I think of it, I'll be wanting the video cassette recorder to tape programs for me while I'm away. I may be traveling quite a bit.

There's the week in Hawaii and the week in Paris, plus the jaunt to New York for a $5000 shopping spree. There's also a trip to Colonial Williamsburg which includes first class round

34

trip transportation from the major airport nearest my home and one week's deluxe hotel accommodations for four persons, subject to availability. (Presumably of the hotel, not the persons.)

In this instance, I'd consider taking the $7500 cash alternative. If I still want to go to Colonial Williamsburg, I can drive and stay in a cheap motel, or at least fly tourist and pocket the difference. I would enjoy flying first class — those seats look so comfortable — but if I take the money, I can spend a few hundred dollars on a really comfortable chair to put in the living room of the vacation home of my dreams and sit in it anytime I want.

Although it lacks the glamour of a trip to Colonial Williamsburg, my smartest move was entering the free-meat-for-life sweepstakes. The prize isn't actually real meat. It's $2500 a year for life or $25,000 in one lump sum. This would buy a lot of hamburger but once I've won it, nothing's to prevent me from spending it on anything I like, including a comfortable chair or a trip to Colonial Williamsburg. The trick here is to figure out exactly how many more years I'm going to live, multiply by $2500, and compare the amount with the eventual yield on $25,000, wisely invested. I'll admit it's a tough problem, but I intend to call in a good financial planner to help me.

One of the most appealing sweepstakes I entered is awarding a reunion for a family of ten. I don't have a family of ten but if I win, I'll take applications for new relatives. I'd like to add a grandparent or two, and perhaps an eccentric maiden aunt — the independent type who wears tennis shoes and travels alone to India. The sort of woman Katherine Hepburn plays would be nice. Or Katherine Hepburn herself. I'm sure she'd like my family.

Since there's no straight cash involved, this sweepstakes doesn't have the investment potential of the others, but it does include a $5000 family shopping spree at the store of our choice. Of course, we'd take Kate along. I'm sure she'd like to go. She probably doesn't get many invitations to go shopping because everyone assumes she's busy. When we're done shopping, we can go back to the vacation home of my dreams and watch *The African Queen* on my VCR.

Yet another company is vying to bring my family of ten together. This one, however, offers a cash alternative of $15,000. I know it sounds cold but this is my investment program we're talking about, Kate. If I win this one, I'm going to have to take the money. Please understand. Fifteen grand is a lot to give up just to smile at you over a turkey dinner. You're still welcome to come over and watch *The African Queen* anytime, though. Just call first to make sure I'm back from Hawaii.

YOU GO ON WITHOUT ME
(I'll just eat here)

Once upon a time there were no picnics. People ate outside all the time, but that was only because there was no inside to eat in. The discovery of fire turned every meal into a barbecue, but still there were no picnics. Only after the invention of dining rooms (or at least kitchens with eating space) did picnics make their debut.

A meal is a picnic only when there is no good reason to eat outside. If, for example, you are stranded alongside the highway and decide to eat your cheese sandwich to keep from fainting while you wait for the tow truck, you can't call it a picnic since you are not there by choice. Put simply, a picnic is a meal eaten outdoors by an otherwise intelligent and responsible adult who had the option of eating indoors but chose, against all reason, not to do so.

Of course, you won't find that sort of elucidation in the dictionary. Mine (a 1979 edition of *The American Heritage Dictionary of the English Language,* since you asked) limits its definition to "a meal eaten outdoors on an excursion," which really doesn't tell the whole story. The second meaning, "an easy task or pleasant experience," not only doesn't tell you very much but makes absolutely no sense since picnics are neither easy nor pleasant.

Take, for example, the problem of chairs. Generally speaking, there are no chairs at a picnic. At best these are backless benches which threaten you with splinters in inconvenient places.

The only way to have a proper chair at a picnic is to carry one along, which seems silly when there are plenty of chairs sitting at home in your dining room where you could have eaten if you wanted to. Besides, you already have your hands full with a cooler of beer, a bucket of chicken and a bowl of potato salad which you are in danger of dropping in the parking lot. With all that, how in the world do you think you're going to carry a chair, too?

The main reason you need a chair on a picnic is because if you don't have one, you have to sit on the ground, which, of course, is dirty. Lacking a chair, you'll need to bring a blanket along to spread on the ground, just one more thing to carry with the beer, the chicken and the potato salad, so you might as well bring a chair.

While you are carrying the beer, the chicken and the potato salad from the car and looking for a place to set up your chair or spread your blanket, the beer and the potato salad are getting warm while the chicken is getting cold. By the time you are sufficiently arranged to eat, the temperatures of all the elements of your meal will have met at a uniform lukewarm.

Uninvited guests of the phylum *Arthropoda* , order *Insecta,* are as plentiful at a picnic as chairs are scarce. Most typical are flies, which are partial to cold chicken, bees who are fond of warm beer and ants who are attracted to potato salad at any temperature. Now, perhaps you have flies, bees and ants in your dining room. If you have, I suppose you might as well eat outdoors, provided you can solve the chair problem. But if you haven't, you should seriously question your motives for this whole venture before you drop the potato salad in the parking lot.

If, indeed, you really like warm beer, wouldn't it be much simpler just to take a trip to England?

YOUR GENERIC CRITIC REVIEWS EVERYDAY ESTABLISHMENTS #1

Ed Snediker's Full Value Hardware in Westlake really lives up to its name. Along with a plentiful array of fasteners and electrical parts, this delightfully unassuming emporium serves up a lot of pleasant extras: bins of loose screws along the back wall, a full line of drain traps and free yardsticks with "Snediker's Full Value Hardware" printed on not one, but both sides.

I tried the combination lock with spin dial, while my companion selected a pre-cut redwood birdhouse. Both were nicely presented and the birdhouse, on an early special, was a real bargain. On another visit, a member of our party got the half-gallon of special tough-duty paint and varnish remover in the no-drip container. While generally pleased with the preparation, he found it to be slightly over-packaged and somewhat lacking in aroma. The only real disappointments among Ed's regular stock are the security chains and self-stick house numbers. Word from behind the scenes is that efforts are being made to bring those departments up to the level of the rest of Ed's.

Long a neighborhood tradition, Snediker's is just being discovered by trendy east-siders with a craving for real hardware. On weekends, you may have to stand in line to get in, but it's worth the wait. One warning — this is not a hangout for nuts and bolts dilettantes. You won't find any plastic bubble packs at Ed's. The folks who go to Snediker's Full Value aren't there to be seen; they're there to buy hardware. We give it three and a half (3½) stars.

We also visited Russell H. Beekman, DDS, in the Heights Medical Center this week.

The real problem here is lack of imagination. Dr. Beekman's offerings have hardly changed since we first reviewed this dental establishment when it opened six years ago. Standard fare predominates: cleaning, fillings, extractions, partial bridges, crowns, dentures and the ever-present root canals. Although he's recently added molar implants and acrylic bonding, it just isn't enough to lift Beekman's out of the ordinary.

This lackluster assortment is further hampered by extremely poor service. On one visit, in spite of having made a reservation, we waited nearly fifteen minutes before the receptionist showed us to our chair. The decor at Beekman's is consistent with the other aspects of the establishment: adequate, but undistinguished, although the antique periodicals on the corner table are a nice touch.

Overall, Dr. Beekman's is a disappointment. If you're in the neighborhood, all right, but we really can't recommend it. We give it only one and a half (1½) stars

Another tip — the house mouthwash here is strictly domestic. Unless you happen to have a taste for it, better stick to water.

———————————

SUGGESTIONS

NUCLEAR WEAPONS FOR PEACE AND QUIET

It's the destructive force we've all been waiting for: sound seeking missiles. This nuclear dream-come-true launches automatically when any sound above 92 decibels enters its field. Equipped with a finely-tuned internal guidance system, the SSM homes in on the sound and destroys the source. Particularly sensitive to heavy metal, it can take out Twisted Sister from a distance of three miles.

Recent small-scale testings of SSMs at a suburban shopping mall resulted in the elimination of seven ghetto blasters in less than three minutes. Trial runs at area parks have been similarly successful, ridding broad areas of Madonna and Duran Duran, along with bothersome insects.

Congress is expected to vote next month in favor of a major appropriation which will fund the installation of SSM silos on the corners of all major intersections throughout the country. Any car passing with its windows open and radio on full would be instantly neutralized. Estimates are that the incineration of as few as 17 battered Chevy Novas would be sufficient to provide a deterrent to further sound environment abuse.

Although orginally developed as a tactical weapon for use in the fight against rock music, this multi-purpose warhead has also been proven deadly to Barry Manilow songs, Muzak arrangements of Beetle tunes and "The Ride of the Valkyries" if played before 8am. In addition, if desired, it can be adjusted to incinerate anything with an electronic percussion track, including leisure-suited cocktail lounge organists playing samba music with a "black box drummer."

Also worthy of government expenditure is the development of smaller SSMs for domestic use. Such a device would find a ready market among the parents and older siblings of

12-year-old girls. As the only viable defense against hearing "Like a Virgin" 27 consecutive times, in-house nuclear warheads would establish an appropriate balance of power and assure that demands to extinguish the stereo would be met promptly.

SSMs could also be a tremendous boon to apartment and condominium dwellers. A discreet decal on the door of your unit lets others know that your suite is equipped with sound seeking nuclear warheads and insures a peaceful building. If your explosive device is still intact when you are ready to move, your security deposit will be returned by the management. The missile lease then transfers to the new occupant of the unit.

It's the next step for civilization: nuclear weapons for peace . . . and quiet.

A VIOLIST
BY ANY OTHER NAME
(would be more interesting)

With the exception of trumpet players and drummers (and they do tend to be exceptions), all symphony musicians normally are referred to by the names of their instruments followed by the suffix *-ist*. Adhering to this formula, one who plays the viola is a violist, one who plays the flute is a flutist, and so on.

In addition to releasing an alarming quantity of sibilants into the atmosphere, this is excruciatingly dull and offers no insight into the personalities of those so designated. "Flutist" reveals nothing at all about the flute player and "violist" tells little about the individual other than the fact that this person has chosen to make a life's work out of reading a clef no one else understands.

In service in the broader world of non-musical employment are a variety of occupational suffixes, including the common *-er* (as in waiter), *-y* or *-ey* (as in nanny or jockey), and so on. These assorted endings could be put to good use within the orchestral ranks, thereby both relieving the monotony and providing interesting information about the musicians.

Some possibilities, in roster order, include:

violiner — a string player from an East German city, as in, "Ich bin ein Violiner"

violint — violinist with little regard for the condition of his suits

violer — string player from the Big Apple

bassey — cross-over artist; plays jazz as well as classical repertoire

flutrix — flying, female flutist

obess — fat double reed player who belongs to a religious order

bassooner — double reed player from Oklahoma

contra-bassooner — double reed player from Texas

cornetress — long haired cornet player
euphoniumian — polite name for a rude horn player
tromboney — extremely thin lower brass player
bass tromboner — brass player given to making crude errors
tuber — potato-eating brass player
harpy — you'd be crabby, too, if you had to tune 46 strings
         every time you wanted to sit down and play
triangler — percussionist whose hobby is fishing
cymbalist — musician who finds deep meaning in 473 bars of
         tacit.

How to Be Sick
and
Stay Home from Work

Being sick and staying home from work is a woefully underdeveloped art. Infused as we all are with the so-called Protestant work ethic (specific religious affiliations aside), our usual response to illness is to continue to drag ourselves to the office until we can neither work effectively nor stay home gracefully. This sort of "crisis reactive" approach to sickness eliminates all trace of finesse from the activity. In order to raise our standards, a few guidelines are necessary.

When to be sick

Experts agree that being sick on a Monday lacks credibility and is therefore seldom appropriate. Regardless of the true nature of your malady, if you are out sick on a Monday everyone will assume you've exceeded your weekend party quotient. Avoid being sick on a Friday. In addition to being accused of copping a long weekend, you'll miss the T.G.I.F. celebration after work.

Unless absolutely necessary, being sick on a Wednesday is never a good idea. An absence on a Wednesday leaves you with a week composed of two Mondays and two Fridays, obviously too much for anyone to endure. Such a hardship could make a person truly ill. The best day to stay home from work is Tuesday. Being sick on a Tuesday gives you a chance to come in Monday and check the weekend mail. When you return on Wednesday (or Thursday), you'll have a short week and Friday will be there before you know it.

If Tuesday is not possible, your second choice should be Thursday. Thursday's only detraction is that you already will have worked three days and may be too tired to enjoy being home sick. (Being home sick on the weekend is such a waste as to be unworthy of discussion.)

Choosing your illness

You'll want to avoid anything too serious. Being really ill takes all the fun out of staying home sick. A good rule of thumb is to stay clear of any illness that keeps you awake or spoils your appetite. Diseases that involve excessive dripping, coughing or sneezing fall into this category. Severe headaches and anything else that may affect your eyesight also should be avoided. Such conditions could interfere with television watching and novel reading, two stay-at-home activities second in importance only to eating and sleeping.

A mild fever is strongly recommended. It's easily controlled with aspirin and lends a ring of authenticity to your illness. Moderate aches and pains also are good, as is a rash, so long as you can identify where you got it and are certain that it *will* go away. If you're athletically inclined, a minor injury is a pleasant alternative to the usual infectious diseases. Something like a pulled thigh muscle or a sprained ankle can be sufficient to keep you in bed while leaving the rest of you quite comfortable.

If you feel absolutely awful, it's best to go to work. (How can you possibly enjoy staying home when you feel so bad?) Take along cough medicine, tissues and plain aspirin. After transferring the aspirin into a large, dark prescription vial, arrange the three items across the front of your desk and suffer visibly. For those deprived of observing your discomfort in person, wheeze and cough into the phone.

How to call in sick

The best way to call in sick is not to call. Have someone else call for you. Logical nominees include your spouse, mother, son, daughter, aunt, grandfather, roommate or, if you live alone, a neighbor. Try to select a caller who is appropriately sympathetic and will employ descriptive adjectives. If available, a friend with some background in community theater might be a nice choice. Be sure to instruct your caller to be vague concerning your immediate prospects for recovery and your eventual return to work.

Should you find you must place the call yourself, try to have audible symptoms. Partial laryngitis is always effective, as is overwhelming nasality. If you plan to employ coughing, you may wish to warm up before dialing.

When your absence is due to a non-communicable condition such as the minor injuries described above, an eyewitness from your office is a must. Here you should make the call yourself, simply saying that you're not feeling well and won't be in. Try to sound brave. Your witness then can regale your co-workers with stories of your bravery, detailing your selfless sacrifice in pursuit of the company bowling championship (or whatever).

What to do while you are home sick

There are four activities fundamental to staying home sick. The first, of course, is eating. This is not the proper time to worry about counting calories or balancing carbohydrates. After all, you have to get your strength back. Try to remember to stock up a few days before you are going to be sick so that you will have an ample supply of foods necessary to your convalescence. In addition to the near-mythological chicken soup, chocolate doughnuts and pepperoni pizzas have been known to work wonders.

Your next consideration should be rest. When you are home sick, lethargy is not only permissible, it is therapeutic. After calling your office, go back to bed. Before dropping off, you may want to set your alarm so you can wake up in time to have lunch before your afternoon nap.

Watching television while you're home sick affords your mind the same respite sleep provides your body. It is important to watch only shows that are a complete waste of time. Soap operas are the most suitable, with locally produced talk shows a good second choice. Game shows are permissible only if you can refrain from trying to answer the questions.

Reading materials should be carefully selected several days in advance. (Stop at the library or the bookstore on your way home from getting pizza and doughnuts.) Recommended are paperback romances, non-intellectual detective novels and the trashier offerings of the best-seller list.

Being sick and staying home from work can be rewarding if properly planned and executed. As with any skill, it takes practice. Studies indicate that the majority achieve their goal within one flu season. Only proper attention to detail is necessary to make the transition from crude collapse to creative malingering.

THE HOLIDAY
EQUALIZATION ACT

The second day of October, with fall barely wet behind the leaves and Halloween yet to come, 20 Santa Clauses piled onto Lolly the Trolley and careened about the streets of downtown waving and ho-ho-hoing to call attention to the American Heart Association's sale of holiday greeting cards.

No doubt some self-appointed preacher will decry their early appearance, chiding us all for mundane materialism and warning against the dangers of empty secularism. Some other nostalgic souls will betray their age by musing about a time when Christmas didn't start until the day after Thanksgiving.

Tinsel now blooms as early as November 1 in many parts of the country, possibly from climatic changes due to the greenhouse effect, but more likely, as just another element in the trend to year-round Christmas. At the moment we have Christmas for three months, one quarter of the year. It's a step in the right direction but we could do better. With proper planning and appropriate legislation, we could celebrate not the 12 days of Christmas, but the 12 months of Christmas.

As with your license plate renewal date, your designated holiday time would be determined by your last name. Those whose names begin with A or B would have Christmas in January. Families whose names start with C and D would celebrate in February and so on. Modern married couples who maintain separate surnames may register either as their Christmas name, or they have the option of celebrating twice which, with their two-career yuppie income, they certainly could afford if they weren't spending so much on a nanny.

A holiday equalization, standardization and normalization act establishing a 12-month Christmas could have tremendous benefits for our sagging economy. It would even out cash flow for boutiques, caterers, and greeting card companies. It would stabilize the twinkle-light trade and improve the market for fruitcake futures. Airlines could charge holiday fares all year 'round and department stores could increase customer traffic by running after-Christmas sales at the end of every month.

A year-round Christmas would mean school and church choirs could save rehearsal time by singing the same Christmas music all year. The Grinch would steal Christmas at 7:30pm the first Tuesday of every month and Perry Como would have full employment for the first time since he left the barber shop.

"Why can't we have Christmas the whole year around?" asks that sentimental old song. We can . . . in fact, we're already working on it.

———————

TENNIS, EVERYONE?

L ike the selection of colors Mr. Ford offered to Model T buyers, current tennis scoring provides no options. Whether you're using add or no-add scoring, either you take the point or you don't. Miss the shot and you've got nothing to show for it, no matter how hard you've tried.

For example, if your opponent drops a shot into the corner diagonally opposite the one in which you are standing, you are likely to hurl your out-of-condition body across the court, only to reach the point of impact a millisecond too late to return the ball. Under current scoring rules, you recieve nothing at all for that effort.

A more flexible system would permit a greater variety of responses to tennis situations other than you get the point/you don't get the point. The above described circumstance might be rewarded with an extra half point because, even though you didn't manage to hit the ball, you did get to it. You expended the same effort and gained the same aerobic benefits as if you had actually arrived in time to hit the ball and, after all, you're doing this for the exercise, aren't you?

Additional compensation is appropriate should you reach the ball and manage to get your racquet on it, regardless of where the ball goes after you hit it. Your risk of coronary is the same whether you hit the ball in or out. A minimum three-quarters of a point would seem equitable.

A successfully completed shot that involves running backwards should be worth twice as much as one that only requires you to run forward. And a volley returned backhand should be worth more than a simple forehand drive. Give yourself two points for the backhand and one for the forehand, unless it involves squinting into the sun. Then you should take

1½. If you are left handed, backhands are probably easier for you to hit than forehands because you've been doing everything on the wrong side for so long, therefore you should reverse the system.

A backhand shot that you have to run backwards to get should be worth at least four. If you hit it at all, no matter how wildly, it counts for 2½, unless it goes into the net. Then you should only take 1¾ because you're going to get a chance for a small rest while you saunter forward to pick up the ball.

If you are over 40, you receive a bonus of one-quarter point whenever you are required to move quickly. If both you and your opponent are over 40, the older player gets one-quarter point for each year advantage the younger player has. For example, if you are 43 and your opponent is only 41, you get an extra one-half point whenever the game requires you to break into a run.

This system, as illustrated, provides for creative response to a number of situations encountered in a tennis game and can be tailored to suit individual circumstances. Just be sure to work it all out with your opponent ahead of time to avoid the possibility of heated arguments on the court. At your age, neither of you has any energy to spare.

———————

REALIFE MERIT BADGES
FOR
GROWNUPS

C hildren have numerous opportunities for positive reinforcement. In kindergarten they get gold stars for such
accomplishments as inhaling and exhaling or sitting
down by bending their knees. When they are older they get
smile faces on their papers just for spelling the words right and,
if they are in scouting, they can earn merit badges in everything
from leatherwork to atomic energy.

Grownup Scouts of America recognizes that Emmy
Awards, Pulitzer Prizes and Federal research grants are beyond
the reach of the majority of adults. Most grownups are unable
to get any recognition for their accomplishments except in the
form of a paycheck, and the government is quick to take the
joy out of that. Believing that positive reinforcement is
necessary for personal growth, G.S.A. has developed Realife
Merit Badges for Grownups to reward adults for their everyday achievements.

To qualify for a Realife Merit Badge in COPING, complete
three of the following activities:
1. Change a flat tire on a busy street during slushy weather
without saying anything that would make your mother faint.
2. Call the repair shop about your new VCR that chewed up the
rental cassette of *Purple Rain*. Do not get a headache when you
learn that the warranty expired last Tuesday.
3. When renewing your license plates, invite three friends to
stand in line with you. Take a picnic lunch. Plan the menu and
shop for food yourself.

To receive a Realife Merit Badge in OPTIMISM you must
be able to do all of the following:
1. Eagerly open the registered letter from the IRS believing that
they wanted to be certain you got your refund promptly.

2. Answer the telephone at 3am without assuming someone has died.

3. Walk confidently downtown after dark, sure in your knowledge that the young man following you for five blocks is a Guardian Angel interested only in your well-being.

To earn a Realife Merit Badge in IMPROVISATION, demonstrate your ability to do the following:

1. Repair a broken zipper using only Scotch tape. Do not cheat and use a stapler.

2. Convince co-workers that the spilled coffee on your suit is part of the fashionable new camouflage look.

3. Scrape the ice off your windshield with a bank card.

4. Five minutes before your guests arrive, prop up the broken couch with overdue library books.

You can earn a Realife Merit Badge in PATIENCE by doing just one of the following:

1. Chaperone a group of 12-year-olds at a roller skating party. Do not hide in the washroom or go home early.

2. Spend an entire afternoon at any suburban shopping mall trying to find a plain, tan raincoat in your size for less than $200.

3. Encourage your uncle to tell you about his army exploits during World War II. Do not stop him when he says, "Stop me if I've told you this one."

Completion of any two of these activities within a three-month period qualifies you for a masochist's ribbon to be worn on your uniform above your pack number. Completion of any three earns the gold martyr's pin. Junior high school teachers are automatically awarded the masochist's ribbon, as is anyone who voluntarily prepares a turkey dinner more than once a year.

To earn a Realife Merit Badge in PHYSICAL FITNESS, complete all of the following requirements:

1. Plan to begin exercising faithfully every morning beginning tomorrow. Do this for 14 days.

2. Every Tuesday for one month, walk down the stairs from your office instead of taking the elevator. (Do not do this if your office is on the ground floor.)

3. Stand up and sit down eight times consecutively without

cracking your knees. Do not rest betwen repetitions.

4. Test your fitness level by watching aerobics on PBS. Practice until you can watch for the entire half hour without sweating.

NOTE: Before beginning this or any exercise program, check with your physician.

To qualify for a Realife Merit Badge in PERSONAL GROOMING, successfully complete the following requirements:

1. Wear matching socks every day for a week.

2. Put your belt on without missing any of the belt loops. Do not let anyone help you.

3. Clean all the cat hair off your navy blue suit with masking tape. Moving quickly, get out of the house before more than 30 percent of your suit is re-covered with cat hair.

DISMISSED, DISGRACED AND DISMANTLED

Medical malpractice is a hot topic. Slick magazines devote their covers to it and national network news presents special reports on the subject. These investigations have brought forth a number of important questions, not the least of which is: when found guilty of professional misdeeds, how are doctors to be dismissed from their profession? A lawyer found guilty of misconduct is disbarred, while a member of the clergy would be defrocked for similar wrong-doing. What happens to women and men of medicine who misbehave?

An obstetrician might be delivered, a podiatrist, defeated. If the offending physician were a surgeon, his colleagues certainly would cut him off. A neurosurgron would probably just be unnerved. An orthopedic surgeon who strayed would be disjointed, a cardiac specialist, disheartened. However, a general practioner who ran afoul of the law would just be bagged.

Such misconduct within the realm of academia might result in language teachers being declined or possibly denounced. Geometrists would be delineated and an errant philosopher most surely would be decanted.

In the artistic community, composers would be denoted and music theorists diminished, while opera stars would be unsung. Orchestra conductors would be beaten, authors written off and Shakespearean actors barred. Among visual artists, painters would be brushed off, weavers unraveled, quiltmakers dispatched and potters fired. A photographer would no doubt be exposed.

In the trades, ill-behaved electricians would be delighted and plumbers flushed. A mason most certainly would be delayed, while a landscaper would be defoliated and a tree surgeon relieved. Printers would be depressed and chefs deranged, while a labor leader would be disorganized. Tailors would be divested and coatmakers dismantled. Lumberjacks would just split.

Ballplayers found guilty of professional misdeeds would be debased, while jockeys and track stars would be erased. A flasher might be debriefed and, of course, cowboys would be given the boot.

A secretary who didn't behave would be defiled, a banker disinterested and a loan officer discredited. A reprobate accountant would be deducted and a teller withdrawn. Unprincipled movers would be dislocated and landlords released, while undertakers might be disembodied. Florists who stray could expect to be deflowered, and manicurists, like secretaries, would be defiled. A hairdresser would be distressed, a masseur rubbed out.

Public servants would not be immune. Firefighters who committed crimes would be extinguished, traffic cops defined, and postal workers delivered.

Out in California, errant vintners would find themselves deported and in Tennessee, moonshiners would be dispirited. A guilty sharpshooter would be dismissed while a munitions expert would be detonated.

Possible punishments for writers who disgrace their profession could include punctuation and sentencing. Most, however, while doubtless deserving of harsher punishment, would simply find themselves described.

Today's
Blue Light Special

More and more potential parents are waiting longer and longer to have fewer and fewer children. In their pursuit of corporate and material success, many are postponing parenthood, adding babies to their households only after the warranty on the second Cuisinart has expired. Few, it would seem, have noted the substantial fiscal benefits they are by-passing by remaining childless.

The first and most obvious is the income tax deduction. Under the current tax law, you receive a deduction of $1080 for every child. If you have two children, still a nice number, you save $2160 every year at tax time.

Children are cheap to feed. To begin with they don't eat very much at all. As they grow older their appetites increase but their food preferences tend to cluster at the low end of the cost scale. Hot dogs, a favorite food of younger persons, cost only about $1.89 a pound. Compare that with steak at $4.00 a pound. Most children, given the choice, would eat hot dogs for supper five or six nights a week. At a savings of more than $2 per meal, that's $10 saved on meat every week, a hefty $520 a year per kid.

With your steak you would no doubt choose to drink a moderately priced but pleasant California burgundy at around $6 a bottle. A child, however, will choose imitation fruit-flavored powdered drink mix at 22¢ a quart over burgandy any time, a savings of $5.78. Assuming you have wine with dinner 1½ times a week (not unreasonable, given the pressures you're under at work), you could save $450.84 a year.

Children are not only cheap to feed at home, they're a real bargain when you dine out. Most restaurants offer child's portions at half of what an adult dinner costs. Given an average entree price of $8 at a family restaurant, and assuming you still have two kids and that you eat out once a week (twice the week between Christmas and New Year's), you've saved $424. Start taking them out as soon as they can eat solid food and by the time your two children are 16 and 18 years old, you will have saved $12,720 in restaurant meals alone.

You save money on entertainment, too. A movie costs at least $4 today, but children can get in for only $2. Take both of your hypothetical children to the movies every Saturday (except the week between Christmas and New Year's), and before you know it, you've saved $204.

The list of fiscal benefits of parenthood goes on and on. Send yourself on a cruise and you're looking at better than $2000, not including airfare. A child can go to camp for less than $500, a $1500 savings. Where you might demand a decent seat to the orchestra for $18 or more, a child is content to stay home and watch free cartoons on television — a $452 savings if you subscribe to a 12 concert series.

Of course, you'll want to discuss it with your accountant, but the facts speak for themselves. In these days of high prices, you really can't afford not to have children.

CRUMBLING
THE
CHRISTMAS COOKIE

I t happens to all of us. No matter how good our intentions, no matter how well we plan for the holidays, there always seem to be some things that don't get done. Each year we vow anew to find time for all those little extras that make a holiday special like spray painting the cat with green glitter or upholstering the garage door with red velvet, but inevitably we come up short.

Even though Christmas is almost here, there is still lots of time to not bake cookies. In fact, one of the most pleasant ways to enjoy this busy seaon is to get together with some other people who aren't baking cookies and have an exchange party.

Here's how it works.

Each guest brings the recipe for a special Christmas cookie that she didn't bake this year. It may be an old family favorite like the sugared turnip gems that your mother's sister Rena used to make every year even though no one ever ate them or it may be a cookie like molasses cranberry coconut drops that no one would consider baking in the first place. Other good varieties to not make are the Mexican crescents that contain a week's salary in crushed pistachios or those anise cookies that take nine operations spread over 72 hours. Each guest should try to not bake a different kind of cookie so that there will be a nice variety.

If your family doesn't happen to have any particular Christmas cookies that you traditionally don't bake, there are a number of excellent sources for cookie recipes you won't be tempted to make. Look on the label of a can of sweetened condensed milk. You're sure to find something there that you won't want to bake or eat.

Check the spiral-bound collection titled "Cook-Ease" that

you bought at the church bazaar for treasures like Mildred Fitzler's No-Bake Goodie Lemon Bars, made of leftover popcorn, peanut butter, lemon gelatin and Mildred's secret ingredient, two tablespoons of Italian salad dressing. Seasonal food ads in women's magazines yield recipes for sweet potato brownies and marshmallow mayonnaise jumbles, either of which would be a wonderful choice to not bake. In the same issues you'll find articles that feature cookies containing ingredients like essence of rose water or preserved lichee nuts which certainly someone in your group will want to not make.

Just for fun one person might bring a recipe from the cookbook her four-year-old's preschool published. (Break eleven-teen eggs. Dump in some salt and sugar. Mix it a while and cook two minutes. Your mother will tell you when it's done.)

Caution everyone to bring sufficient recipe cards to share with all the other guests so everyone can go home with a good selection of recipes for cookies she's not going to make. Be sure to include the full directions and baking times so that you'll all know how much time you're saving by not baking these cookies. After you swap cards, talk about how much fun you're having not baking Christmas cookies. Tell each other what kinds of cookies you plan to not bake next year. Then rip up the recipes and go buy some Christmas cookies.

———————————

BRAVE NEW WORDS

The year 1984 has come and gone and little has changed. Big Brother may be watching us but Newspeak never caught on as the universal language. The little words of wisdom that guide our lives are pretty much the same as they've always been but our needs are different. We need some new sayings that suit our modern situations. We need up-to-date axioms that address the issues of the moment. We need Brave New Words, proverbs for the '80s that we can apply to all the important areas of our lives like:

Financial planning —

A fool and your money are soon partners.

Home is where the mortgage is.

Where there's a will, there's a relative.

There's no accounting for the IRS.

The environment —

May showers kill April flowers.

Still waters smell bad.

Where there's smoke, there's Los Angeles.

Medicine —

Patients are a virtue.

An ounce of prevention isn't covered by your policy.

Physician, insure thyself.

Denistry —

Nothing dentured, nothing stained.

Economics —

What goes up is never your salary.

A penny saved is worthless a year later.

Nothing is certain but death and tax shelters.

Commuting —

All roads lead to construction.

The early bird gets caught in rush hour traffic

Don't cross the bridge until you come to the toll booth.

Government —

Old soldiers never die; they just double-dip.

Washington loveth a cheerful giver.

Media —

Good news is no news.

Where there's life, there's *Time, Newsweek* and *U.S. News and World Report.*

If you can't say something nice, call *The National Enquirer.*

Travel —

Time flies when you're headed east.

The longest journey begins with a single airport security check.

When in Rome, LOOK OUT.

Entertainment —

All that glitters is Liberace.

Sports —

The bigger they are, the more money they get.

The green is always grassier on the other side of your slice.

He who does not keep pace with his companions has his Walkman tuned to a different station.

Contemporary living —

Children should be seen and not rented to.

The darkest hour comes before the power is restored.

A barking dog always lives next door.

Beauty and fashion —

A stitch in time saves face.

If the shoe fits, it's not your color.

Half a loaf still has more calories than none.

Relationships —

Mothers are an invention of necessity.

A friend in need never loses your phone number.

All the world's a stage that we're hoping to grow out of.

PLANT PARENTHOOD

No one talks about it . . . but one of the most serious problems facing suburbia today is zucchini proliferation. Squash control advocates have been distributing free literature outside of garden supply stores and lecturing at libraries in an attempt to remove the social and moral stigma through education. Nevertheless, unwanted zucchini continue to be a source of embarassment in many communities.

A surplus of zucchini can have a substantial negative impact on a neighborhood. Early in the breeding season residents often are lulled into thinking that they are immune to the devastating effects of cucurbit oversupply. The ritual sharing of squash with nongardening neighbors may even create a false sense of camaraderie on the block.

Recipients of this misguided bounty begin to lose their humor by late August but maintain decorum, politely declining their gardening neighbors' gifts. By Labor Day the social order shows signs of strain. Squash-weary neighbors hide behind the drapes when a gardener approaches. Crazed by the omnipresence of squash, backyard farmers begin leaving baskets of dark green, torpedo-sized zucchini on front porches. The unbidden appearance of these containers causes property values to plummet. Driveways develop cracks, screen doors hang from their hinges and the neighborhood enters a decline.

Voluntary contol is not realistic, given the Mediterranean proclivities and low educational level of most zucchini. Squash of all varieties are known to wantonly cross-pollinate with any other available cucurbit. The most morally undeveloped of vegetables, zucchini will play around with anything that has a vine.

The most effective method of zucchini population reduction is the quick and merciful disposal of the adult plants before they have the opportunity to set fruit. Although cucurcide (the legal term for such action) is condemned as harsh by some, it is kinder than allowing these plants to produce unchecked, ultimately to endure the heartbreak of seeing their offspring wasted on the compost heap.

———————————

Rent-a-Relative from Holiday Ambiance

F amilies are getting smaller and smaller every year. More and more people are staying single, and those who do marry are having fewer and fewer children. There aren't as many great aunts and uncles around as there used to be, and everybody's grandparents have retired to the sun belt.

A holiday table with only you, your dog and the widower from down the street who makes strange noises into the stuffing can be depressing. Plan now to fill out your family for the holidays with Rent-a-Relative, an exclusive service of Holiday Ambiance, Inc.

Perhaps, because of the uncertainty of the nuclear age and the rising cost of quality sneakers, you've made the wise decision not to have children. Most of the year you're glad not to have them underfoot but on Christmas morning you miss seeing those shining little faces gazing expectantly at the gifts beneath the tree.

Well, Rent-a-Relative from Holiday Ambiance can help. Rent one child between the ages of four and ten, get another one for only 50 percent extra. We'll deliver them, complete with jammies and fuzzy slippers, to your doorstep on Christmas Eve, and pick them up the next morning no later than 10am so you can go back to bed. For an additional fee of $153 per child we'll even supply the presents and clean up the debris after the holiday. ($100 damage deposit is required.)

For only $20 more, you can keep the children all day. Take them to church if you like or just keep them around the house until after dinner. Children who eat their sweet potatoes and don't pinch their siblings carry a surcharge of 15 percent. Supply is limited, so order early if you want the well-behaved model. Be sure to specify a child from the WB1500 series.

Maybe you have plenty of children but the rest of your family lives far away. Well, renting relatives for the holiday may be cheaper than what it would cost to fly Grandma here from Sun City. We carry a full selection of retired parents, second cousins, non-judgemental in-laws, and uncles who tell World War II stories after dinner. (Specify smoking or non-smoking.)

This week's special is eccentric maiden aunts who wear tennis shoes and travel to India alone. Order before midnight and save 10 percent. (All major credit cards accepted.)

———————

YOUR GENERIC CRITIC REVIEWS EVERYDAY ESTABLISHMENTS #2

Paper Place on Center Ridge Road has come a long way since it was known as Lenny's Hasty Print. Proprietor Leonard Clutterbuck has revamped his entire operation, bringing in shop foreman Marty Fridl from the coast. That California touch is unmistakable; Fridl's San Francisco-style binding is exquisite.

Available at Paper Place are the printing, copying and folding that Lenny's customers have come to expect. Weekday selections have been expanded to include letterheads, resumes, business cards, envelopes, wedding invitations, and rubber stamps just like the ones we saw on a recent visit to New York. All this plus newsletters, circulars, bulletins and flyers — the variety here is staggering.

Paper aficionados know the best way to judge the talent in the shop is to order a plain paper copy. The one we got on our last visit was just dark enough, enhanced by a little lightness around the edges. Delivered still warm from the copier, it was presented in a Manila folder, simply garnished with an invoice. Though not amazing, it was pleasantly and competently executed.

While the shop doesn't always succeed, the goals are high and the basics are solid at Paper Place. We give it three (3) stars, with an extra half (½) star for imagination, a quality missing in most printing establishments.

Starting next month, Paper Place will offer a Sunday collating service with complimentary coffee from 11am to 2pm. Printers in trendy sun coast cities have had great success with this; whether Lenny can sell it to conservative Clevelanders remains to be seen.

Sam Giannini's Trash Hauling and Disposal Service on Whiskey Island has been on the area business scene since Frank Copella disappeared in 1957, so you can imagine how disappointed we were when we visited it last week. Sorry, but our advice is to skip Giannini's. The place looks like a dump. We wouldn't send anybody but our worst enemy there. No (0) stars for Giannini's.

ONCE
AROUND
THE
CALENDAR

JANUARY

FIT TO BE POLLED

The results are in. Based on an exit poll taken at the World of Weight Loss Health Spa, the most universal New Year's resolution among women is a vow to get in shape. Of those polled, 74 percent admitted this was not the first year they had made this resolution. Fifty-one percent, the overwhelming majority, indicated three or more years of resolving to get in shape. Fourteen percent candidly revealed they had been resolving to get in shape every year for more than five years, and nine percent were in the eight-to-ten year category. The remaining three percent mumbled.

Remorse at overindulgence in smoked liverwurst canapes and/or a surfeit of wassail was the motivation cited by 37 percent. The appearance of svelte second cousins and hyperthyroid younger sisters at family gatherings followed with 32 percent. Twelve percent mentioned recent wardrobe acquisitions in double-digit sizes as having affected their decision, while one woman got a sweatband for Christmas and wanted an opportunity to wear it.

Most of those polled reported having attempted some remedial body work before going semi-public in a leotard. Forty-three percent checked out *The Body Principal* or you-know-who's workout book from the library but were promptly discouraged by smiling photos of Victoria and Jane positioning their bodies in ways proven to produce severe pain in normal women. Twenty-three percent indulged in home weight training using 22 ounce cans of stewed tomatoes and 19 percent began daily jogging but, faced with the realities of January in Ohio, gave up in favor of a trip to Florida, vowing to walk a great deal at Epcot Center.

The majority of first-time fitness resolvers purchased

black and red chevron-striped leotards in preparation for working out, indicating the strong fitness fashion influence of you-know-who. Among the repeaters, however, striped leotards were favored by only nine percent, with 26 percent purchasing Evonne Goolagong cotton blend styles from the Sears catalog, and 43 percent opting for plain black nylon from un-named sources. Twenty-two percent chose baggy sweatpants and faded Fairfield Elementary School T-shirts, claiming the Pillsbury Dough Boy as their sartorial model.

Sixty-eight percent of the women polled had resolved to diet as well as exercise, with most following such plans as Pritikin (26 percent), Atkins (17 percent), Stillman (12 percent) and Arnold Schwarzenegger (five percent). James Coco and Dr. Cooper's Fabulous Fructose Diet each garnered one percent. Thirteen percent were eating to win and 18 percent, having tried on their leotards in front of a full-length mirror, lost an average of 2.3 pounds by crying. Seven percent, all mothers of preschool children, had not eaten a full meal since New Year's Day but were subsisting on peanut butter crusts and trimmings from carrot and bologna sandwiches cut in the shape of Smurfs.

The question of fitness goals proved to be a sensitive issue, with 64 percent declining to reveal the number of pounds they sought to loose. Only four percent would disclose their waist measurements and 58 percent refused to discuss cellulite. The polling was curtailed when one individual, responding to an inquiry concerning her inner thighs, shouted obscenities at the interviewer and assaulted him with a swea-ty leg warmer. Her response was recorded as "no opinion."

FEBRUARY

PURITANISM
WITH
JOCK OVERTONES

A ny sporting goods store manager will tell you. Cross-country skiing is the fastest-growing outdoor activity in the country. Last year a veritable legion of Americans acquired skinny skis, and this season many more are expected to join the rush to the trails. The reason behind this phenomenal growth is that cross-country skiing is not merely a sport; it is a virtue.

Like morals and basic education, virtue had fallen into low regard in recent decades. However, with the advent of herpes and hard times, virtues of all sorts seem to be making a come-back. Feeling smug costs nothing and is easier to achieve than full employment.

All winter sports, the pursuit of which thrusts people in-to the discomfort of winter weather, appear to be virtuous. But not all winter sports are uniformly virtuous, and of the two clearly defined forms of skiing, cross-country is overwhelm-ingly more meritorious than downhill. Like those of us who earn the beauty of springtime by surviving a Midwestern winter, cross-country skiers labor so to reach the top of the hill that they deserve the pleasure of sliding down it. Alpine skiers pamper themselves with the soft hedonism of tow ropes and chair lifts, never earning the delights of their descent. Like liv-ing in southern California, it's too easy to be worthwhile.

Cross-country skiing is Puritanism with jock overtones. There are no slopeside lounges proffering hot toddies and in-stant conviviality. Instead, there is a thermos of tea and a solo granola bar in the backpack. For the cross-country skier, there is no roaring hearth decorated with blond ski bunnies in hand-knit sweaters and genuine Belgian fur boots. Only the warmth of the car heater and the companionship of the car radio wait at the end of the trail.

Alpine skiers posture on the slopes in color-coordinated stretch pants and zippy nylon jackets, surveying the winter wonderland through wraparound sunglasses with someone else's name on them. Cross-country skiers are typified by a wardrobe that would do a bag lady credit. They make their way through the woods in a mismatch of blue jeans, old varsity jackets, sweatpants, generic gloves and odd hats. Fashion (and knickers) may be lacking, but the sincerity is evident. Cross-country skiers are not there to be seen; they're there to ski.

Cross-country skiing is a prudent endeavor. Not for those seeking the empty thrill of foolish adventure, it is a sport of the cautious and the sensible. Cross-country skiers aren't chicken — they're just smart. They are not seduced by the superficial glamour surrounding Alpine skiing. On the downhill slopes, legs are fractured and backs are cracked, but few are injured on the suburban woodland trails. Cross-country skiers know the statistics and decline to play the odds.

Cross-country skiing is also the athletic embodiment of that most unarguable of virtues, thrift. The necessary equipment may be had for as little as one-third the cost of downhill gear. Access to requisite terrain is most often free to cross-country skiers, while Alpine aficionados squander their cash on lift tickets. When the low cost of the previously described cross-country apparel is considered, to say nothing of what you save on toddies, the sport begins to inch over the line from thrifty to downright cheap.

Then, too, there is an appealing element of efficiency in cross-country skiing. With skiable terrain at the doorstep, there is no need to fly to Colorado or drive to New York. No long weekends, vacations or time away from work. The cross-country buff can rise early, ski for an hour (an hour that no doubt would have been wasted in slothful slumber) and still get to the office on time. The energy savings realized by staying in the neighborhood make the choice of cross-country over downhill a patriotic gesture as well.

All these sterling qualities, however, pale beside the renowned benefits of cross-country skiing as physical exercise. It is so unutterably healthy! With self-torture in the name of physical fitness fast emerging as our preeminent national value, cross-country skiing has taken its place right up there with other socially sanctified forms of misery, such as jogging, racquetball and that masochism to music, aerobic dance.

A complete exercise, cross-country skiing provides superb muscular conditioning and toning. The substantial cardiovascular benefit is illustrated by the huffing and puffing of skiers as they gasp for breath. A valuable aid to weight control, the activity consumes 550 to 700 calories per hour, depending on the size of the skier. Moreover, the lifestyle engendered by cross-country skiing encourages the establishment of good weight-control habits. How much can a person gain on one granola bar and no toddies?

Perhaps the true key to the popularity of cross-country skiing is to be found in the psychological aspect of the sport. There is a feeling of individual power and strength, of total well-being that is significant to the enjoyment many find in the sport. Known as the "skier's high," this phenomenon is the addictive euphoria which frequently overtakes dedicated skiers as they shush along the trail, faces red, noses dripping, lungs whimpering for oxygen. As the high begins, the skier achieves new depths of psychic awareness. He feels incredibly healthy. He feels overwhelmingly smug. He feels intolerably virtuous . . . just before he collapses.

MARCH

MEMBERSHIP WEEK ON WMTE

You're watching WMTE, viewer-supported meat eater's television. [ring, ring . . .] We know that you tune in to WMTE for special programming that you can't get on the networks . . . like the program you were just watching, "The A-1 Team with Mr. T-Bone."

Because of their limited appeal, these programs can't be offered on commercial television. There simply aren't enough meat eaters anymore to provide a large enough audience for them, but we can bring them to you here, on WMTE, your carnivorous station . . . arts programming such as the traditional jazz special we brought you last week with Saturated Fats and the Hydrogenated Five, fine daytime dramas like "As the Spit Turns," and everybody's favorite, "The Butcher."

You'd pay for these fine programs on cable, but here on WMTE, viewer-supported meat-eater's television, we bring them to you free. [ring . . .] Just three times a year we appeal to you, the coronary prone, to help us keep these programs on the air. A membership in meat eater's television is only $30, barely the cost of one spiral-sliced half ham. And for your $30 you get not only the satisfaction of knowing that you're helping to keep meat eater's television on the air, you get our monthly program and recipe guide. [ring . . .] Call now and you'll also receive this beautiful booklet on the Heimlich maneuver, with an introduction by All-Star Cook.

Are you one of the thousands of viewers who tuned in for all 12 episodes of "The Jewel in the Crown Roast" on Mister Please Theatre? Then make your pledge now. We need your support. [ring . . .]

You know, so often I run into people by the pork loins at the supermarket who say, "Gee, I just love your programs ... "Lifestyles of the Rich and Overweight," "That's Inedible," and the new "Name That Casserole." But when I ask if they're members of meat eater's television, they say, "Well, you know, I was meaning to call and pledge but I never got around to it." Well, now's the time. Let's get these phones ringing. We know you love our programming because you tell us so but without your support we can't stay on the air.

Please ... if meat eater's television is important to you, as I know it is, call now and make your pledge — before you have that coronary. And now, let's get back to our programming. Here's a special treat that I know you're going to love [ring ...], back to back, four vintage episodes of "Calling All Carnivores." [ring, ring ...]

APRIL

THE ANNUAL, AUDIBLE JOKE COUNT

Each year on April 1, thousands of dedicated joke watchers across the country volunteer their time to spot and record jokes. The raw data are then sent to a central location for collation and interpretation, the resultant information being used by humorologists to study the migration of jokes and further our knowledge of their habits.

It is still a mystery how a fledgling joke, offspring of two mature Polish jokes in Patterson, New Jersey, can make its way unaided to Hibbing, Minnesota in 48 hours, regardless of the weather. Records from past joke counts show that it is possible for a joke, no matter how weak, to cross the continent in less than a fortnight. Major routes of migration are associated with industrial sales representatives and weekend family phone calls, with certain joke species showing a preference for employee newsletters or late night television.

Some species of jokes not only migrate but exhibit cycles of hibernation. In the temperate zone, light bulb jokes hibernate on an annual cycle while elephant jokes, like locusts, are dormant through most of their 17-year life span, emerging only to breed. Polish jokes, the dominant group in this region, are active year-round.

Habitat plays an important part in the distribution of joke forms. Puns flourish in proximity to concentrations of computer programmers, science fiction writers and choral conductors. Wife jokes, extinct in most parts of the country, have been found thriving in isolated pockets around V.F.W. posts.

There is strong evidence that certain mental wastes damage the humor environment. The effluent produced by bank loan officers and municipal clerks is extremely toxic to small quips. Puns have a difficult time breeding in areas where large amounts of illiteracy have been released into the air by urban society. In addition, mutations such as the jokes that roost on after-dinner speeches force out more delicate species, making it difficult for them to compete.

Organizations dedicated to humor conservation contribute greatly to the preservation of the country's humor heritage. Their work has included the banding of double entendres and the construction of nest boxes for shaggy dog stories. Several groups are now urging the creation of a national system of satire sanctuaries. The information collected each year through the April First Audible Joke Count contributes immeasurably to our understanding of jokes, resulting in increased awareness of and respect for our nation's precious humor heritage.

MAY

CLEANLINESS IS NEXT TO MOTHER

I n my mother's house, cleanliness was not next to godliness. It wasn't even close. Godliness, I suspect, she could take or leave, but cleanliness was right up there at the top of her list.

My sister and I washed before we sat down to eat, a precaution against bearing germs to the table. And just in case we were sticky, we scrubbed again at the end of the meal. Before leaving the house, we washed our hands and faces and brushed our hair, and we washed when we came indoors from playing, so as not to leave fingerprints about. All of this sudsy activity didn't seem obsessive to me. It was merely part of the matrix of well-ordered routines that formed the structure of our lives.

My mother harbored a deep belief in the curative powers of cleanliness. No matter what the affliction, she prescribed the tub. "Take a bath," she would say. "You'll feel better." Tired and irritable? Take a warm bath. Hot and sticky? Take a cool bath. "You'll feel better." Cold and sneezing? A hot soak and a cup of tea was the answer.

My mother's faith in the medicinal powers of bathing was utterly unshakable. She applied her favorite remedy to all of the usual childhood diseases. I bathed my way through three-day measles, 14-day measles, mumps, scarlet fever and an assortment of colds and flu. I may have been spotted, speckled and sniffly, but I was clean. Whatever the malady, Mother would pop me in the tub to soak while she laid out fresh pajamas and remade the bed with smooth sheets, clean pillowcases and soft-smelling blankets. "You'll feel better," she'd say, and I always did.

As I grew older, soap and water were applied to the psychological struggles of adolescence. Mother's answer to the doldrums was a scrubbed face and maybe a clean shirt. The worst bouts of adolescent ugliness were treated with cleanliness and the crying jags of my teen years always concluded with Mother recommending, "Now, go in and wash your face and brush your hair. You'll feel better."

The restorative values of cleanliness were not lost when I went away to college. In need of revitalization while overdosing on knowledge, my friends would break for coffee and a cigarette. I would regain my senses by washing my face and brushing my teeth. At the end of finals week my teeth would sparkle and my skin would be peeling.

Cleanliness is still the answer to many of life's tangles. When I have absorbed too many negatives in one day, I head for the shower and wash the tension down the drain. I take my troubles to the tub and soak out whatever is bothering me, and a hot bath is always my first response to an approaching illness.

The established habit of applying soap and water to difficulties also serves my work. Overwhelmed by a passage that refuses to come together, I push away from my desk and head down the hall. After I brush my teeth, wash my hands and comb my hair, I return to the problem refreshed.

It doesn't usually help, but I feel better. And it reminds me of my mother.

JUNE

TRAVEL TALK

A lmost everyone will be going on vacation sometime this month or next. In order to assist you with the planning and successful execution of your trip, this week's "Marginal Considerations," with a nod to the various perpetrators of myriad similar guides, is devoted to some of the more common travel terms and their nearest English equivalents.

Ratings of accommodations, for example, are given in a sort of code. "Standard accommodations" means only one towel. "Deluxe accomodations," two towels. "Luxurious accommodations," two towels and a miniature bar of Ivory soap. All the amenities? The television works.

When you're on vacation, you don't just eat — you dine. "Fine dining" indicates you can get ice cubes in your water if you ask. "Leisurely dining" means the service is slow. "Casual dining," the service is slow and the waiter tells you his first name.

"Complimentary cocktail" means three ounces of spiked fruit-flavored punch in a paper cup. "Complimentary champagne cocktail," three ounces of spiked orange-flavored punch in plastic wine glass. "Meals include unlimited wine" means vintage: Tuesday.

Conveyances are similarly coded. "Motorcoach," of course, is bus. "Deluxe motorcoach," bus with clean windows. "Superdeluxe motorcoach," bus with clean windows and a lavatory.

Adjectives relating to atmosphere and location are especially tricky. "Sun-drenched" translates as desert. "Ocean breezes," constant gale. "Tropical," a nice steady rain, and 'invigorating" means it's too cold to go swimming, even in August.

"Quaint" equals shabby. "Old world charm," the bathroom's down the hall. "Historic," in need of renovation. "Relaxing pace," boring. "Off the beaten path," not right on the freeway. "Secluded," two miles from the freeway. "All the comforts of home," you can get ice cubes in your water if you ask. "Playground of the stars," Gerard Hoffnung stayed here once.

In reference to shopping, "charming local crafts" means bird feeders carved from coconuts. "Unbelievable bargains," the bird feeders carved from coconuts are cheap. "Duty-free shopping," you may bring home as many bird feeders carved from coconuts as you like.

"Options galore," everything costs extra. "Explore on your own," pay for it yourself. "Nominal charge," outrageous charge. "Affordable," you can always mortgage your home.

"First name in travel," AAAAA-1 Tours. "Other attractions too numerous to mention," three things, none of which will interest you. "Dedicated staff," you can get ice cubes in your water . . . if you ask.

JULY

REALIFE SUMMER CAMP FOR GROWNUPS

This summer Grownup Scouts of America is again offering Realife Summer Camp for adults. Available in both day and sleep-over programs, Realife Summer Camp can make the summer a time of personal growth for your grownup, while keeping him or her off the street.

Realife campers participate in a wide variety of sports activities such as hiking at the mall and swimming in a crowded municipal pool. Camp arts and crafts include building your own Heathkit bug zapper and alphabetizing spice cans. You may want to crochet pink and green covers for spare rolls of toilet tissue or try your hand at repairing a snow blower using parts cannibalized from an old 2½ horsepower outboard motor.

Nature study is an important part of camp life. At Realife Summer Camp, grownups unlock the secrets of nature and learn how to feed mosquitos, why fried chicken and potato salad attract ants, and how to kill grass organically and safely, using only dandelions, chickweed and dooryard plantains.

Educational day trips add variety to the camper's experience and include fun-filled jaunts to the dry cleaners, the automatic bank teller machine, and, weather permitting, the peradontist. A special all-day field trip to an area shopping mall gives campers an opportunity to work toward completion of the requirements for the Realife Merit Badge in conspicuous consumption.

Food at the Realife Summer Camp mess hall is wholesome and delicious. Three balanced meals a day plus an evening snack are prepared in the Realife institutional kitchen by vacationing elementary school cafeteria workers. Many

90

campers use their week at camp to work on Realife Merit Badges in dieting or tofu.

No summer camp would be complete without campfires. Each evening at sunset, Realife campers gather 'round the gas grill for sing-alongs and cookouts, and, on the last night of camp, the annual mock PTA meeting.

For a summer of memories, call your local Grownup Scouts of America office for more information on attending Realife Summer Camp.

AUGUST

BETWEEN
JULY AND SEPTEMBER

True, it's hardly perfect. It has heat and humidity and, in some locales, mosquitoes, but of the selection of months currently in stock, August is one of the better models.

Contrary to its customary detractors, August has much to recommend it. August weather, for example, is a paragon of reliability. Unlike such fickle months as April and November, August offers weather that is trustworthy and consistent. It is always hot. Occasionally hot and dry, more often hot and sticky, but always predictably hot.

The August heat, aside from its innate dependability, is possessed of many virtues. It provides a perfectly logical excuse for lethargy that at other times of the year would be taken for mere sloth. It allows for the happy continuance of such folk rituals as the annual feature-page photograph of an egg sauteing on the sidewalk. And as without the dark we would not appreciate the light, without the August heat we would never know the exquisite pleasure of stepping from the sultry mugginess into an air-conditioned restaurant on those nights when it's "too hot to cook."

August is unhurried. A late entry in the annual lineup, August didn't join the calendar club until 46 B.C. No doubt it arrived several centuries after most of the other months because it just didn't move very fast. Along with July, August nestled in at the end of the summer, ultimately forcing Sextilius into retirement. Before everything was settled, the Emperor Augustus, with stereotypical imperial vanity, purloined a day from poor February and tacked in on the end of his namesake so as not to be bested by the other Caesar's month.

On the long side as months go, August is replete with

time. There's never much to do in August. By August it's too late to initiate more plans for the summer and too early to adopt autumnal hyperactivity. Most things cultural are off-season. Nothing is on television except reruns of programs that weren't worth watching the first time. Every second person is on vacation and the wheels of commerce and government roll forward at a more leisurely pace.

August is non-judgmental. In August it is possible to lie on the beach and not even pretend to read. Indolence is acceptable in August. August is fruit salad and tuna fish for dinner and no one really cares, as long as there's enough iced tea. Householders who in June fanatically clipped and manicured the lawn adopt a *laissez faire* approach toward the ever-growing August grass because, after all, it will only need to be cut again.

By August there's nothing much left to do in the garden. Most everything that is going to die has done so and the rest is growing so rampantly that nothing could possibly stop it. Flowers and vegetables alike are past ripe, obscene in their profusion and promiscuous in their yield. A feast for the body and fine food for the eyes, vermilion tomatoes, emerald peppers and amethyst eggplants all are attainable with little effort in August.

August's most sterling quality, however, is the utter absence of holidays within its bounds. It is this unique attribute which sets August above and apart from all other months. There is in August not a single ordained occasion of celebration or commemoration. There are no special events to attend, no obligatory rituals to endure and no traditions to defend. None of the remaining 11 yearly segments is so blessed. For 31 wonderful days we need muster neither ceremonius solemnity nor artificial frivolity and not once in all of August are we forced by some decree to survive our Monday on a Tuesday.

Other months expect so much. July always insists on at least one massive gathering of the clan around a smoking barbeque pit while in August, family picnics are deemed optional. August demands no presents and no resolutions. August requires no greeting cards, no decorations or parties of any kind. Never in the entire month of August are we intimidated by the advertising media around us into purchasing flowers, boxes of candy, plastic pumpkins or green beer. For the length and breadth of August we can skirt the shopping mall, shun the boutique and avoid the florist without guilt. August is a binge of non-consumption.

August is as it is with good design. Without the uncluttered expanse of August, we could not face the frenetic rigors of fall. August is an extended furlough, a megadose of rest and relaxation to bolster us on that upward haul to winter. Through the torpid days of August we store away energy to be summoned at a later date. As the light fades, we draw upon it, redeeming the value of those unstructured hours. Up autumn's incline it carries us, over the summit of the seasons, and onto next spring's giddy downhill run to summer.

———————————

SEPTEMBER

STUFF THE ZUCCHINI

J ust as the first crocus signals the coming of spring, the end of summer is told by fried zucchini. And baked zucchini. And steamed zucchini, boiled zucchini, broiled and stuffed zucchini.

In a frantic effort to use the surplus fruits of these indiscriminately prolific plants, homemakers produce quantities of such aberrations as zucchini pickles, zucchini pancakes, zucchini applesauce and that ultimate perversion of natural Midwestern thrift, zucchini bread.

Zucchini bread is an invention requiring the misguided expenditure of two eggs, one cup of sugar, a half cup of shortening, one and a half cups of flour, a half cup of raisins and occasionally nuts, plus small amounts of assorted kitchen staples like baking powder, cinnamon and salt, at a total cost of more than one dollar, so as not to waste one cup of utterly worthless grated squash. Thousands of kilowatts of valuable energy — enough to run the hair dryers of a mid-sized European state for 11 days — fuel the baking of these loaves. The resultant product (without the nuts) is about 2,700 calories — approximately 225 calories per slice, of which fewer than three calories are squash.

People who make zucchini bread make it not only for their own use, but to give away. Throughout the harvest season, they go around passing out loaves like Jesus feeding the multitudes. Every second loaf gets tucked away in the freezer, there to lurk among the ice cubes like a cheap fruitcake, ready to be called into service as an impromptu Christmas gift for some unsuspecting holiday caller.

Should you receive several loaves of zucchini bread (and if you live within 17 miles of a gardener chances are good that you will) you needn't feel that eating them is your only option. Loaves of zucchini bread serve well as doorstops and bookends. If baked in those cute little individual-sized pans, they make chic paperweights. Sliced lengthwise, they are useful as patio bricks.

Hollow out the bottom of one loaf and hide your valuables in it. Convert another into a clever lamp for the rec room. Throw several loaves in the trunk of your car this winter to improve traction. Construct bohemian bookcases of unfinished boards supported by stacked bread. For a rustic effect, use bread baked from unsifted whole wheat flour.

If your surplus zucchini are in their raw vegetable form, there still are any number of interesting things you can do with them. Have a zucchini bronzed and hang it from the rear-view mirror of your RV. Glue off-white parchment around one and use it as an artificial fireplace log. Fence your yard with zucchini, choosing either picket or split-rail style.

Dress up a zucchini in discarded clothes and, like a nine-year-old with a Cabbage Patch Kid, take it everywhere with you. Don't call attention to it, and refrain from introducing it to anyone. You'll still be noticed. Store the largest zucchini in a cool dry place until spring and prop it up in the garden to frighten next season's young plants into infertility. Save several others to hollow like dugout canoes and fill with pink and white variegated petunias. Suspend them from your porch railing.

Choose a nicely shaped zucchini and, using a No. 3 hook and two contrasting colors of cotton yarn, crochet a cover for it, alternating rows of shell stitch and double picots. Display the finished zucchini on the back of the commode in your powder room. Make an unusual Halloween decoration by scooping out a zucchini and carving facial features and other anatomical details, as you see fit, on the resultant shell.

Be aware that pursuit of some of these suggestions might create social difficulties for you. Your block club may even circulate a petition requesting that you move out of the neighborhood. However, compared with actually eating all that zucchini, ostracism seems a kind fate.

OCTOBER

TRICK OR TRADEMARK?

I n the autumn of playgrounds past, the query of "who did you get this year?" was soon replaced by "what are you going to be for Halloween?" It was a question of elementary-aged existence second in importance only to "what are you getting for Christmas?"

Through the month of October, ideas were bandied about at recess to be refined in the crucible of peer-group opinion. (Oh, boy, is that dumb! Frankie wants to be a spider from outer space. Boy, are you stupid, Frankie!) Once past the review board of contemporaries, costume plans were tested on mothers for feasibility. (Tin foil won't work for a magic silver cape, Doreen. It'll tear before you get as far as the Stedmans' house.)

Fantasies were played out and career ambitions articulated by the identities chosen for the occasion. Asthmatic boys with negligible musculature looked forward to masquerading as football heroes. Plain little girls plotted their impending transformation into beautiful princesses-for-a-day, while future surgeons of America dug toy stethoscopes out of cardboard medical bags and secured grinding masks from the hardware store.

Ghosts, witches, skeletons and vampires materialized perennially in never-ending variations, no two quite alike. Cowpokes and hobos, America's mythological figures, were equally inevitable and every year, one child with a clever mother would show up as a pumpkin, green leotard legs sticking out of the bottom of a bulbous orange body of Rit-dyed cheese cloth stretched over a coat hanger frame.

While the girls gravitated toward fairy tale princesses and ballerinas, the boys showed a preference for tougher identities.

Bums were created with old flannel shirts and too-big trousers held up by suspenders. A bad guy was attired in a borrowed trench coat and an old felt hat, pulled low. Characteristic of a bad guy was a heavy five o'clock shadow of charcoal and, if the bad guy's mother would allow it, an unlit cigar stub clenched in the teeth.

Nationality costumes were popular because they were easy to assemble. Dutch girl required only a blue dirndl, a white blouse, an apron with red tulips drawn on it, and one of those winged hats folded out of white paper. Spanish girl called for the same white blouse, a full skirt of red or orange, and a black lace shawl to be draped mysteriously over the head and shoulders. Hawaiian girl was achieved with a bathing suit topped by a crepe paper skirt and several cellophane leis from the Lions' Club Carnival. The effect, however, could be endangered by a climate-conscious mother insisting on a cardigan sweater being worn over the bathing suit.

There were beasts and creatures, too. Insects had extra limbs sewn to the sides of their jerseys. Crepe paper-winged butterflies took flight with pipe cleaner antennae atop their bathing cap heads. Ducks with rubber swim-fin feet and pussycats with eyebrow pencil whiskers stalked the sidewalks.

Sometimes, the choice of disguise was influenced by the availability of a ready-made costume. An older sibling's hockey uniform or cheerleading skirt could be pressed into service. An Oriental identity was likely if a cousin serving in Korea had sent home a black silk kimono with a multi-colored dragon embroidered on the back.

Embellished with a bit of makeup and topped off by a half-mask of white or black satin, these annual disguises were temporary mobile monuments to imagination. Store-bought costumes were considered hopelessly second-rate to such custom-scrounged outfits. (Also regarded with utmost scorn were costumes designed to serve as night wear after the holiday. In any era, kids know leopard print flannel pajamas when they see them.)

"What are you going to be for Halloween?" still is hotly discussed by the playground set. Today's answers, however, all have trademarks and proper names. Television and movie characters have edged out cowpokes and hobos. Darth Vadar and He-Man are today's tough guys, while the girls choose Princess Leia or one of several versions of the durable Barbie.

Instead of a robot, there is Dr. Doom, and goblins have been uppercased to Gremlins. Brand-specific Smurfs and Care Bears have replaced generic witches and ghosts, and instead of one inevitable pumpkin, every block turns out a half-dozen Strawberry Shortcakes.

True, today's mothers are short on cheese cloth dyeing time and fathers have yet to step into the home sewing arena in large numbers, but that's really incidental. What's at work here is the same force that causes ten-year-olds to demand jeans with someone else's name on the backside. The child who wears a non-copyrighted costume is beyond the pale.

Today's fantasies are predefined and limited to those packaged identities offered for sale. Halloween outfits come from the shelves of discount stores, not attics. They are manufactured in Taiwan and distributed by a company in Brooklyn, and every store has an identical array. A universe of possibilities has been reduced to a multiple-choice list . . . and while it may be something small, doesn't it seem as if something has been lost?

November

Thought for Food

All of us heard it. "Eat your dinner. There are children starving in China." Depending on the age and ethnic background of your parents, the starving children who dominated your table conversation may have been in India or Europe instead of China. No matter. Your folks could have told you there were children starving on Mars — the results would have been the same.

First you tried to reason with them, pointing out that your eating or not eating a plateful of disgusting liver and brussel sprouts would have no effect one way or the other on the children starving in China/India/Europe. You may even have volunteered to mail your liver and brussel sprouts to the first starving Chinese/Indian/European whose zip code you could find, possibly throwing in that you would gladly pay for the postage out of your allowance. Unless that got you a one-way ticket to solitary confinement for being a smart aleck, ultimately you bowed out of the situation by feeding the liver to the dog and stuffing the brussel sprouts in the back pocket of your jeans.

Nobody who is reading this has ever been hungry. Not really. True, we burst through the door at the end of the day with "What's for dinner? I'm starving!" but it's just an idiom, an inaccurate figure of speech. "Starving" is not a word that has any real meaning for us.

Our problem is not a paucity of food but the misuse of it. On any given weekday, more than 50 percent of American women are dieting. (Add another 20 percent on Mondays and days following holidays.) Nutritionists are forever telling us to ingest less fat, less sugar, less salt, less red meat, less cholestoral, less alcohol, and more fiber, more vegetables, more whole grains. Seventy-five percent, they say, of our total calories should come from vegetable sources.

As it is, three-quarters of our grain, used to feed animals who process it by their own time-perfected secret formulae, turns up later on our plates as London broil, quiche and moo goo gai pan. One pound of animal protein costs over 20 pounds of vegetable protein to produce. It seems obvious that there'd be a lot more food to go around if we ate the grain directly instead of feeding it to the cows first.

In a world where many cannot get enough to eat, eating cheaper food and less of it should be a moral act. Theoretically, my supper of brown rice and vegetables will free up grain resources and increase the world food supply. In reality, it will only cause American beef producers to throw more money into advertising to fight declining sales.

We do not need our mothers to remind us that children are starving in Africa. In this month of Thanksgiving, as we prepare to celebrate our wealth we are acutely aware of their privation. Yet, anything we might do would have about as much impact as eating our liver and brussel sprouts would have had on the children our mothers said were starving in China/India/Europe. Something is wrong.

Cutting back on calories may reduce our waistlines, but it will not increase the African food supply. It is sad. But the fact that the delivery system is flawed doesn't get us off the hook. The obligation remains to eat more responsibly, not to waste, not to eat what we do not need. If nothing more, to do so may keep us aware of (and possibly grateful for) the opulence we take as normal, and aware of a painful problem still to be solved.

Sending to Ethiopia the money we save by not eating steak may help a hungry child, but not very much and not for very long. Still, it is something, and we must do it . . . if not for their undernourished bodies, then for our starving souls.

DECEMBER

OH, YOU REALLY SHOULDN'T HAVE (really)

Y ou've probably done most of your gift shopping by now. You may even have the packages wrapped and under the tree. But don't let yourself be misled into thinking that your job as a gift-getter is completed. The most important part of the process still remains: that of evaluation. How well did you really do with your holiday shopping? What's your success rate as a gift buyer?

"Oh, you really shouldn't have" almost always means you really shouldn't have. "Fantastic" is a pretty good indication that you probably made a good choice, unless the recipient is a sports announcer or writes ad copy for a living. Then all superlatives have to be discounted.

"This is marvelous" probably means that the recipient really does think it's marvelous, unless the first syllable is drawn out, as in, "This is *mar*velous," in which case either she's a community theater actress or she intends to exchange your gift for something purple.

"Excellent" from a teenager is a high rating. Give yourself good marks for this one. The same goes for an unsolicited "Wow" spoken by any child under ten. If the child says "Thank you very much, it's just what I wanted," he's been coached. Although it may be just what his parents wanted you to buy for him, it isn't just what he wanted and you should make a note never to buy the kid anything like that again.

"Lovely" from an adult female means she may like the present but has three of them in her dresser drawer already. "How nice," or "Very nice, thank you dear" indicates that you really blew it and she's wondering why in the world you would buy her such a dumb present. If your gift is greeted with "How interesting" or "What a unique gift," you've strayed too far into the esoteric. He hasn't the faintest idea what it is and you're going to have to figure out a tactful way of explaining it without embarrassing him by acknowledging that you know he doesn't know what it is.

"Well" and "Now, *that's* a present" are reserved for items so incredibly ugly, inappropriate or ludicrous that even the best-bred are hard pressed to come up with anything more positive. If your gift gets one of these, you're probably beyond hope. Maybe you should just give everybody cash next year.

———————

YOUR GENERIC CRITIC REVIEWS EVERYDAY ESTABLISHMENTS #3

For Myra, lead hairdresser at the Turneytown Beauty Spot, it's been a very good year. With her three back-up operators, Myra has made a place for herself at the top of the industry, with several of her cuts going platinum. The shop's June and July performances attracted record crowds and every seat in the house was booked the afternoon we were there.

Myra opened with a shampoo. The tempo was brisk, the rhythm quick and upbeat, a perfect beginning. She followed the shampoo with a rinse, a conditioner and another rinse in rapid succession, a threesome that has become a programming standard for her. Here Myra displayed her instinct for pacing, changing the mood from hot to cool and back again.

The cut that came next was a classic. All the elements were there — straight bangs, rounded sides, and the characteristic gently tapered back. Beginning slowly, Myra took her time with the material, working with it carefully until, at the very end, the beauty of the form was clear. Although the Dutch Bob has been done by virtually every artist in the business, in the hands of someone like Myra, it's worth one more cover.

Winding up the performance was Myra's curling iron which we've seen before but could never, ever tire of. A quick trip to the hairdryer was followed by a brief reprise of the curling iron which added just the right embellishments to finish off the set in style. We give Myra four (4) stars. What an operator!

Our next stop was the Great Northern location of Carpet Heaven where manager Nigel Cusp continues to prove that floor covering does not have to be dull. Customers who haven't visited the outlet in a while may be surprised. Nigel has recently rearranged his showroom to emphasize the minimalist forms of the boxed tile. By juxtaposing the severe lines of the vinyl self-stick squares with the opulence of rolls and rolls of multi-level shag carpeting, Nigel creates a strong statement very expressive of the decadence of our age.

Often described as an analytical abstract expressionist, Nigel now is leaning toward realism with a touch of the surrealistic. Gone is the American primitivism he previously affected, and all the braided rugs, once so prominent in Carpet Heaven's displays, have been discounted and moved to the chain's warehouse. In their place are works of continuous filament nylon, monolithic rolls of synthetic plush, and some exemplary Ultron. With these Nigel seems to be accepting a newly discovered aesthetic in which technology and art are no longer exclusive.

For as far as it goes, the display is a successful one but there is just so much one can say with select multicolor cut loop and nylon saxony. One hopes that Mr. Cusp, having resolved his personal conflicts about man-made fibers, will now begin to take a broader approach to his materials. Carpet Heaven earns three (3) stars.

MOSTLY
TRUE
STORIES

THE KAPELLMEISTER
OF
KAPIOLANI PARK
(See Hawaii, Places to Visit)

I had gotten the volume from the shelf in order to determine roughly when the craft of knitting ceased to be the province of male guilds. A small detail for an article on the domestic arts, easily and quickly located in the encyclopedia.

Klipspringer (see Antelope). Klondike, Knee, Knife, Knighthood. Inadvertantly, I flipped one page past my goal and was distracted by Knots. Temporarily forsaking my quest of Knitting, I became immersed in the subtle distinctions among knots, hitches and splices. Fascinated I wended my way through intriguing diagrams of intricate twinings with picturesque names. Cat's Paw. Carrick Bend. Eye Splice. Memories of my Girl Scout handbook. Tuck strand A through first, then strand B, as shown. Turn the loop over and tuck strand C through. Then tuck each strand through twice more.

Recovering my proper sense of purpose, I turned back, still in search of Knitting, and discovered that the Kittiwake is a gull that gets its name from its plaintive cry. Kittiwake, kittiwake, kittiwake, it cries. I gave it a try. "Kittiwake, kittiwake." Somehow it lacked plaintiveness when I did it. Perhaps the individual gestalt of the gull adds emotional content to the expression. The adult kittiwake, by the way, is 16 to 18 inches long.

Thoroughly seduced by this aggregation of alphabetized knowledge, I browsed through Kings Canyon National Park and Kiowa Indians. Colorful photographs of Kites captured my glance and a Kinkajou stared out from the page with big monkey-sad eyes.

Odd juxtapositions abounded. Kern, Jerome David, was duly biographed opposite Kerosene. Kalamazoo shared a column with the Kaiser. Khrushchev's angry upraised fist was followed shortly by Kidney Bean.

I leafed to Khachaturian, Aram Ilich, a Russian composer who was influenced by folk music he heard in his early childhood. Had he been named Key, Francis Scott, instead of Khachaturian, Aram Ilich, he might well have been a child prodigy. As it was, Aram no doubt was so busy listening to folk music and learning to spell his name that he had no time for composition until a more advanced age.

Keohuk Dam, one of the largest power dams in the Middle West, caught my eye, but I was led astray by Kale and Kohlrabi. Koala Bear next absorbed my attention, only to yield to Kaki (see Persimmon). Keratoconus (see Contact lens). I wondered at the connections. Kola. I always thought it began with a "C". Kilmer, Joyce. Another surprise. The author of *Trees* was not female. My inability to utilize the encyclopedia efficiently was becoming painfully evident.

Surrendering all pretense of my stated mission, I embarked on an expedition from Kenya to Kentucky, to Kansas, Korea and Katanga, 'round to Karachi and back to Kerrville, Texas, by way of the Kuril Islands. En route I tarried with Kennedy, Kosygin, Kafka and Krupa. I chatted with Sandy Koufax, Grace Kelly and Danny Kaye. After studying a Kandinsky painting, I made it halfway through the Krebs Cycle before stopping to rest beneath a Kapok Tree.

Sitting on the floor in front of the bookcase, weighty tome balanced across my knees, I mused on the pitfall to which I has succumbed. Through the writing of third-grade reports, high school term papers and college theses, I had exhibited this same character flaw. Even today, I am equally untrustworthy with a dictionary or thesaurus, inevitably straying on my way to the entry pursued.

Resolute now, I turned to Knitting. *NIHT-ing,* "a way of making an elastic, porous fabric from yarn by means of special needles." Further definition. Methods of knitting, explanation of the two main stitches (knit and purl), and three common knitting patterns (garter, stockinette and rib). The piece of information I needed was not to be found, although 1589 was mentioned as the date of the first stocking firms in England. I would have to go to the library after all.

Meanwhile, did you know . . . the Kouprey lives only in Cambodia ... a Kudo is a large antelope ... and Komonder is a breed of large shaggy dog that the Magyars brought with them when they invaded Hungary in the 900s ...

MORE THAN JUST REAL ESTATE

F or nearly two years I passed the house on my daily commute. In the evening, when the lights were on, I would slow down, trying to see into the windows as I drove by. Several times I considered stopping. I thought I might just knock on the front door and ask to look at the house. "You see," I would say, "my grandparents — my father's mother and father — used to live here."

I worried about how I might offer assurance that I was harmless. "I just want to see if it looks the same as I remember it," I would tell them. Maybe I would write a note first, giving them references so they could verify my identity and feel confident I was not trying to gain access to their home for some shady purpose. The appearance of a "For Sale" sign on the lawn solved my potential credibilty problem. I called and made an appointment to see the house.

This house on Lake Road is the setting for 50 percent of my childhood Sunday recollections. The other 50 percent lie in the opposite direction on Lake Shore Boulevard in Euclid. Nearly every week after church my family motored either east or west along the shore of Lake Erie to visit one or the other set of grandparents.

I remember my grandparents' house in Lakewood as big, quiet and cool. Oak trees littered the front lawn with acorns that I took home for my "science collection," an ever-changing assortment of natural flotsam arranged on a TV tray in my room.

This is not an ordinary house. In bad weather we disembarked from the car protected by the elegant portico that extends over the driveway. The fireplace at the far end of the living room is flanked by wrought iron sconces that echo the design of the dining room chandelier, and between the two rooms are wrought iron gates which my sister and I delighted in closing to "lock in" the grownups.

The cook's pantry linking the dining room to the kitchen contains a wealth of cupboards, shelves and drawers, sure seduction for someone like me who swoons over storage systems. Beyond the kitchen, with its own bathroom and separate entrance, is the maid's room where I liked to stay as a teenager, pretending I was on my own in a London flat.

The house oozes gentility. The master bedroom is distinguished by a fireplace in the cozy sitting area. To the back of the room is a private screened-in porch, to the side, a walk-in dressing room with built-in drawers and cupboards. (The dressing room opens on the other side to the back hallway so as to permit the maid to put the laundered and pressed garments away without disturbing the occupants of the bedroom.)

Against all logic, I found myself toying with the idea of buying the house. The seller called me. Would I like to see the house again? The asking price was high — almost 30 percent above the market value as calculated according to standard formulae. Make an offer, he encouraged me. Let's see what we can work out.

Even at a more appropriate price the house would be expensive for me. I shudder to think what it would cost to heat those spacious rooms in the winter. And while I am still captivated by the leaded windows, the fireplaces and the wrought iron gates I fancied as a child, my adult eyes saw signs of water seepage in the basement and noted missing tiles in the back bathroom.

Had this really been the right home for me such things might not have mattered, but I began to see this was not a house I could live in. Shaded by the oak trees, the rooms are cool and quiet, but they are also very dark. I like light and air; this house would close me in. My two very large children are poised on the edge of the nest. They are with me only a few weeks out of the year now. Soon I will need even less space, not more. No, I told the seller. Thank you, but no.

Although my usual route no longer takes me past the

house, I make a point of driving by it whenever I'm in the neighborhood. The sign is down. I assume the seller either lowered his price or found someone with both susceptibility to charm and hefty borrowing power. Perhaps I'll visit the house again sometime. I have to think the new owners won't mind, once I explain. "You see," I will say, "my grandparents used to live here." Surely anyone who would buy a house such as this would understand that houses can be much more than mere real estate. Often they are memories as well.

———————

THE GHOST
OF
CHRISTMAS PRESENTS PAST

W hen I awoke, it was so dark that, looking out of bed, I could scarely distinguish the transparent window from the opaque walls of my condominium. I was trying to pierce the darkness with my eyes when the chimes of my clock-radio struck the four quarters.

Ding, dong. "A quarter past," I said, counting. Ding, dong. Half past. Ding, dong. "A quarter to it," I said. Ding, dong. "The hour itself, and nothing else," I said, yet as I spoke, the hour sounded. Light flashed up in the room upon the instant and the apparition stood before me.

"Are you the Spirit whose coming was foretold to me?" I asked.

"I am," it answered.

"Who, and what are you?" I demanded.

"I am the ghost of Christmas Presents Past," it replied. "Rise and walk with me."

As the words were spoken we passed through the wall and took our place upon an open country road before a spacious home. "Good heavens," I said as I looked about me.

"Do you know this place?" asked the Spirit.

"Know it?" I exclaimed. "My dear sister lives here. Indeed, I know it well, sir Spirit."

"Let us go on," said the Ghost, leading me to the kitchen. There, bathed in a strange light, the counter lay buried beneath a jumble of quiche pans, electric woks and avocado enamel fondue pots. On the stove were piled a crepe maker, hotdog cooker and yogurt maker. A set of eight individual French onion soup crocks spilled from the cupboard. Two fish molds, a springerle roller and a Ronco Seal-and-Save hung on the wall. I recoiled from the sight, shielding my eyes.

"What is the meaning of this, Spirit?" I cried.

"Do you recollect these things?" the Ghost asked.

"But Spirit," I answered, "I have no choice. I can't remember her size. I never know what books she's read."

"Touch my robe," it commanded. I did as I was told and clung fast. Even as I did, we were transported to my parents' hall closet. I stared in disbelief at the hot lather machine, automatic nail buffer and talking bathroom scale on the upper shelf. Stuffed beneath them were two pairs of electric socks (batteries not included), an Australian sheepskin steering-wheel cover and, in the corner, a pink and green hand-crocheted doll whose ruffled skirt hid a spare roll of toilet paper.

Ominously, the Spirit pointed to the doll.

"I meant no harm," I cried. "Mildred Fitzler makes dozens of them every year for the church bazaar. I had to buy one."

"These are shadows of things that have been," said the Ghost. "That they are what they are, do not blame me."

"No more," I cried. "I don't wish to see it. Show me no more." But the relentless Ghost forced me to observe what happened next.

We stood before my uncle's desk and my uncle himself behind it. He was nearly hid from my sight by three acrylic photo cubes, a magnetic perpetual calendar and a cork memo ball. A lava lamp glowed in the dim light. To the side, on the filing cabinet, an aroma disk player dispensed "Northern Pines" at six-second intervals.

"Uncle, dear uncle," I cried. "Can you forgive me? Please, I beg of you." He showed no sign of hearing but continued to pitch paper wads at a basketball hoop affixed to the wastebasket.

"These are but shadows of the things that have been," said the Ghost. "He has no consciousness of us."

"Spirit, you must hold me blameless," I said. "I never know what to get him. He is the man who has everything. Surely you've heard of him. Remove me from this place, I beg you."

Suddenly I was enveloped in darkness. A foul mist swirled about me. "Spirit, Spirit, where are you?" I cried, but no sound answered me. I stumbled through the thick fog to find myself at the curb, in front of my own dwelling. Wordlessly the Phantom gestured to the heap of refuse before us.

Cartons stripped from hot-air popcorn poppers, electronic football games and an automatic dog shampooer were strewn about 'midst a confusion of crumbled wrapping paper, plastic greenery and wrinkled tinsel. MasterCard slips, KMart bags and cash register tapes blew across the landscape. "Before I draw nearer to that to which you point," I said, "answer me one question. Are these the shadows of things that will be or are they shadows of things that may be, only?" Still the Ghost pointed downward with an unmoved finger.

"Spirit, hear me! I am not the woman I was. I will not be the woman I must have been but for this. Next year I will give no one anything bigger than a bread box. Assure me that I yet may change these shadows you have shown me by an altered life." The Spirit was as immovable as ever.

Holding up my hands is a last prayer to have my fate reversed, I saw an alteration in the Phantom's hood and dress. It shrunk, collapsed and dwindled down into a pillow. Yes, and the pillow was my own and the room was my own. I scrambled from my bed, threw back the curtains and looked from my window to the tree lawn below. It was clean, devoid of all trash and trappings. The vision of the night before was gone.

I threw back my arms and declared, "I will buy no unnecessary appliance. I will make no one a gift of an executive toy. I will never puchase another of Mildred Fitzler's crocheted dolls."

And so, as Tiny Tim observed, God bless us, every one. Merry Christmas to all, and to all a gift certificate for the merchandise of his or her choice.

BE PREPARED

I read about it in the newspaper. You probably did, too. The woman merely looked in the phone book and called the number of the first ambulance service that caught her eye. She didn't check around for the best price. After all, she was in a hurry. It was an emergency.

The ambulance service she called proved to be a great deal more expensive than some others she might have reached. No matter, she's stuck with the bill. After all, the ambulance did come.

The woman wasn't prepared. She hadn't anticipated needing an ambulance. She didn't call several services and inquire as to each of their fees, noting which she should call for the best value in an emergency. I've never done that. Neither have you.

From time to time, I think that I should change a tire on my car. Theoretically I know how, but I've never done so on this particular car. I've been lucky. Whenever I pass a poor unfortunate changing a tire at the side of the highway, I resolve to test the procedure in the safety of my own driveway . . . be sure I have all the pieces — jack, lug wrench — and know how to use them. Of course, I've never done this. Neither have you. But from time to time I think I should.

I need a new will. It's been a long time since my current will was written and, as they are wont to do, my circumstances have changed. Now and then, I also think of arranging a low-cost pre-paid burial so my survivors will not be tempted to spend too much money on whatever is left of me.

It occurs to me too that I might draft up an obituary and let my son know where it is filed. I've done a thing or two in my life, and plan to do a thing or two more. I really don't want to go out with just one of those little classified-type notices. Still, I don't seem to get around to doing such things. Neither, I suspect, do you.

I avoid taking unnecessary medication. I pay for car insurance, home insurance and health insurance I hope never to use. I exercise regularly, watch the amounts of cholesterol, caffeine and sodium chloride I ingest, and wear sunscreen on my nose. I don't smoke. I dress warmly and get sufficient rest. I keep a grocery list posted on the refigerator so I won't run out of paper towels or cranberry juice. I save my receipts, file my cancelled checks, put money in my IRA, look both ways before crossing and brush my teeth after every meal. So do you.

There's a microthin line betwen being prepared and fooling ourselves into believing that we really have control over anything other than the most insignificant minutiae of our lives. Last month, an acquaintance discovered a lump in her breast. Within the space of a week she visited her doctor, entered the hospital, underwent a double mastectomy, and returned to her home and family with the knowledge that, despite her surgery, there are cancer cells loose in her body.

Her youngest child is in kindergarten. Surely what seemed important one month ago is not the same as what is important now.

She was not prepared for this. Neither was I.

———————————

MYOPIA, NOT YOURS

I can't see a thing without my glasses. Well, that's not entirely true. I can see blurred blocks of color, occasional streaks of light and vague shapes with fuzzy edges . . . but I can't tell what they are.

Because I'm so near-sighted, it's difficult for me to do anything without my glasses, and those things that must necessarily be done without them are always a problem. Applying mascara is an act of faith and I wash my face entirely by Braille. If I drop the soap in the shower, I'm in serious trouble. The only thing I do really well without my glasses is sleep.

My spectacle wearing affects my behavior in a number of small but significant ways. During the summer, my right hand is in constant motion, pushing up the glasses that are forever sliding down my sweaty nose. In the winter, I walk into buildings backwards to prevent my glasses from fogging up. (It works, but it does cause people to look at me funny.)

Although the wonders of modern optometry permit me to live most of my life in a nearly normal manner, there are some appealing activities that I have found it wise to forego. These pursuits, such as wind-surfing or wet-boat sailing, tend to center around water. Unless fitted with little windshield wipers, glasses simply are not practical attire for such endeavors. And without glasses, I would pose a serious navigational hazard to other craft in the vicinity, as well as a major threat to my own health and welfare. As for swimming, I gave it up years ago because I could never see who was waving at me.

I tried contact lenses. Besides being bothersome and uncomfortable, their use required a quantity of paraphernalia rivaled only by the equipment necessary to perform brain surgery. When wearing my lenses, I needed to be carrying not only lens case and wetting solution, but non-prescription sunglasses (in case I needed to go outdoors), my glasses (in the event I should have to remove my lenses), and my prescription sunglasses (in case I needed to go outdoors after I removed my lenses). It was more than a mere purse could handle. I needed a backpack just for my optical gear.

During adolescence, the magnitude of my myopia lent a whole new meaning to the expression "blind date." Through most of high school I dated a tall, taciturn fellow who was president of the National Honor Society. Tom was his name. In addition to his I.Q., Tom had 20-20 uncorrected vision. I always resented the fact that unaided by artificial means Tom could see and I couldn't. It never seemed quite fair.

Whenever we got into a really serious kissing situation, I would remove my glasses and place them on the dashboard of the car because, somehow, they always kind of got in the way. I guess most people close their eyes when they kiss because it's romantic or because it's difficult to focus on someone so close up. I closed my eyes when we were kissing because I figured I might as well — I couldn't see anything anyway. Of course, I was having plenty of fun with my eyes closed. What bothered me was the idea that if I wanted to see anything, I couldn't. It always made me a little uneasy and I would feel about the dashboard from time to time to determine if my glasses were still there, just in case.

When I was younger, I used to think that I would like to be a redhead in my next reincarnation. And 5'10". Or perhaps look like Audrey Hepburn. With maturity, however, I've changed my mind. Given another go-round at life on earth, I would settle for my present, rather mundane physical appearance. I don't ask for much. Just give me perfect vision, please. After all these years of corrective lenses, my idea of Nirvana would be simply to see where I'm going in a swimming pool.

WHERE THERE'S SMOKE...

A

s an individual, I exhibit the typical profile of an urban pipe smoker: over thirty, upper-middle class, college-educated. Except, of course, I'm female, and pipe smoking in mainstream America is considered to be an exclusively male pursuit. Women do not smoke pipes in our society. Why this should be so is not clear, but it definitely is the case. (Women don't smoke cigars, either, but I take that as mere evidence of simple good sense.)

A cursory and thoroughly unscientific perusal of the literature of pipe smoking reveals that in another time and place I might well have been a pipe smoker. The idle women of the harems of Persia smoked tobacco all day long in water pipes. Accounts of the European explorations of Africa in the sixteen and seventeen hundreds mention pipe smoking women in all parts of that continent. Distaff puffers in Burma, Australia, South America and the Orient also were described.

English women, particularly of the working and servant classes, have smoked pipes off and on throughout history. Ditto for the Irish. Fine ladies smoked tobacco in delicate clay pipes during the time of Queen Anne. Pipes even have been reported in the lovely lips of the monarchy including those of the Dowager Queen of Waganda and Queen Elizabeth, who is said to have enjoyed an occasional puff with her good friend, Sir Walter Raleigh.

My friend Nancy, only slightly older than I, tells me that when she was in college the craze among coeds was tiny pipes decorated with rhinestones. "Not much good for smoking," she recalls, "but extremely effective for shocking parents." Except for Mammy Yokum of Dogpatch, the only woman I can remember ever having seen with a pipe is Yoko Ono, but somehow that's not surprising. Yoko also wrote poems about grapefruit and sold tape recordings of falling snowflakes.

Pipe smoking is said to be an extraordinarily effective means of relaxation. It is a socially acceptable technique for dealing with stress and, unlike meditation, can be done at parties where chanting generally is frowned upon. Knitting, a pastime considered more appropriate for women than pipe smoking, can serve the same purpose but its social applications are much more limited. Although the paraphernalia required for knitting is only slightly more cumbersome than that necessary to pipe smoking, knitting at parties is even more generally frowned upon than chanting.

One of my uncles once owned a pipe. He didn't smoke it, he just owned it. A university professor, he kept the pipe in his desk drawer, taking it out only for faculty meetings. The pipe, he explained, made it possible for him to ignore the proceedings, which usually were somewhat stuffy, and still appear to be attentive.

Men have a tremendous advantage here. A person sitting pipeless, not actively participating in the discussion, appears to be rather dull, or worse, asleep. Put a pipe in that person's mouth and he can be wondering what's for dinner, whether there is life on Neptune or how long it might take to rollerskate down Mt. McKinley. No one will know.

A man with a pipe not only looks like he knows what's going on, he appears to be sagely weighing the alternatives and applying his obviously superior intelligence to solving the problem at hand. Simultaneous with facilitating woolgathering, the pipe also relieves its bearer of the burden of articulate response. He can answer anything with a slow nod and an "Ummmm" or two, and get away with it.

Women have no such ploy to exercise. By virtue of gender, we are denied this most professorial of props. The pipe is not ours to puff profoundly or brandish about in pursuit of a point. We are awarded no lengthy pauses, filled with thoughful scraping and tamping, in which to consider what to say next. Our very best stalling tactic is a discreet doodle at the top of the yellow legal pad or a brief interlude of pencil tapping, not nearly as impressive as scraping and tamping.

Left pipeless by the dictates of social custom, those of us who are female must remain awake and alert for the entirety of the meeting. We have no pipes to invest otherwise unacceptable utterances with legitimacy. We have little choice but to pay attention and speak intelligibly. The men may palm their bowls and stare into space. Ours is to mind the agenda.

OF JACKETS

Poplin jackets, loaded with sporty features for only $11.99. Only $11.99! Smooth polyester cotton poplin. Unlined for lightness. Machine washable, line or tumble dry. Zip closure, two pockets, raglan sleeves. Soft acrylic knit collar, wrists and waistband. Contrasting piping.

I ordered one, size small. I am not a big person. White with blue trim. I am not a flashy dresser. A week later I received a voluminous, bright purple hooded jacket that reached my knees.

The attached packing slip was covered with computer-printed numerals that no doubt held great significance for someone but were meaningless to me. Maybe the stock number of the jacket they sent me was just one digit different from the stock number of the jacket I ordered, an understandable error, I allowed, given the pressures likely endured by the computer-punching order takers. I mean, it could happen to anyone, right? Wrong. The two numbers bore no discernible resemblence to one another. I searched further for explanation.

Off to the left, under the heading "reason for substitution" was a series of little boxes labeled in English: 1.) reorder, 2.) no longer available, 3.) equal value, and 4.) better value. This last was checked. Better value? Someone, somewhere, had decided, for some reason, that a very large, bright purple hooded jacket was a better value for a not very large, moderately conservative woman than a small, plain white jacket with blue trim.

I called the store. The real live person on the other end of the line was extremely pleasant, and not at all helpful. No, sorry, but the store would not pick up the jacket. "Why don't you just bring it in?" she suggested.

But the store is very far from where I live and work, I explained. That's why I have things delivered to my home.

"Oh, dear," she said cheerfully. "That's too bad. They used to pick things up, you know, but they don't do that anymore. It costs too much. Why don't you just mail it back?"

That would cost me money, I pointed out, and it was the store's mistake, not mine. She agreed, and further confirmed that she couldn't do a thing for me. Would I like to write to the main office of the store and tell them what I think of their policy? She offered to give me the name and address of the person to whom I should send my complaint.

Thank you very much, but no thank you. Maybe I'll do that later. Meanwhile, I still needed a jacket.

"Well," she said, "are you a chancy woman? You could just reorder and see what they send you this time."

Under most circumstances I'm not much of a gambler but I figured, hey, what the heck, why not? It wouldn't take me any longer to drive to the store to return two very large, bright purple hooded jackets than it would take to return one very large, bright purple hooded jacket. She put the order through.

I'll let you know what I get.

URBAN REMOVAL

I t was amazing how little time it took — less than eight hours, not even one full working day. They already had begun when I came home from church. As soon as I turned the corner I could see the huge machine filling the street. I could not possibly get to my driveway. I parked the car and walked down the block.

The green house finally was being demolished. Mild weather for November had all the neighborhood out and watching. The wrecking ball danced back and forth, enlarging the wound in the side of the house. The noise was thunderous. We got out the lawn chairs and settled back in the unseasonable sunshine.

Each swipe removed a bit more of the exterior. Now, with one side missing, the building resembled the back of a doll house. The cutaway view exposed a patchwork of painted walls, the chrome yellow, bright aqua and flamingo pink of rental suites, testimony to the landlord's $5-a-gallon attempts at disguising the dinginess. "Newly decorated," the classified always said.

The iron weight swung out and in. Splinters of wood siding and rotted window frames rained down on the late fall mums hugging my fence. The brick walk leading to my front door was covered with thick dust. We retreated to the next yard.

The walls smashed, the vital systems of the house were laid bare. Electrical ganglia and galvanized viscera bristled from the wreckage. The waste stack, a severed intestine, quivered with each blow of the heavy ball. Two kitchens, two baths, three bedrooms down, two up, and a front porch. Shelter for two families.

With a startling thud, the floor gave way and one end of

the upstairs tub dangled crazily through the ceiling. A breeze picked up something left behind — a scarf, or maybe a paper — and floated it over the backyard and into the alley. From across the street came a bottle of wine, and someone passed a bowl of popcorn.

There were always people moving in or out of the green house. Grimy children and yappy dogs came and went. Radios blared from the windows after midnight and Mrs. Demeter called the police.

The tenants would not pay the rent. The landlord would not fix the steps. The housing inspector documented the numerous violations and the owner got an extension from the court. The tenants piled their garbage against my fence in plastic bags that the cats ripped open at night. Mrs. Mahalko called the health department. No money to buy a garbage can till next month's check, said the woman. No money.

Finally there were no more tenants. The house stood empty, bearing silent witness to speculative investment. Saturday nights brought smashed windows and spent six-packs. The neighbors waggled their heads over the fence and the block club circulated petitions. The city inspector reappeared, clipboard in hand, and left to file yet another report, while the landlord hid behind his unlisted number.

I was not yet asleep and no longer awake when Jim came, pounding on my door. "Give me your keys," he said. "The green house is on fire." Clutching my sashless robe together I stood on the steps as he moved my car to the safety of a more distant driveway.

Up and down the street, porch lights blinked on, illuminating nightgowned neighbors. Smoke spilled over my fence. It stung my eyes and sent me inside. Through the window I could see the flames twisting and leaping to the sound of the sirens.

"A strictly amatuer job," said the arson investigator. The inside was unscathed, the exterior only charred. We could smell gasoline. Still, he said, these things are hard to prove. The insurance investigator asked had I seen anyone? What time did I notice the fire? Who turned in the alarm?

As the late afternoon cooled, the neighbors retired to their television sets. Finished with its work, the wrecking crane deferred to the bulldozer. Over the mountain of rubble it lumbered, shoveling the remains in to the basement. Back and forth the machine crawled across the heap of debris, pushing, shoving, breaking it up, tamping it down, leveling it off.

I went inside to get a sweater, leaving rubber-soled footprints in the dust. As I shivered in the dusk, a small truck backed onto the lot, dumped a load of topsoil and drove away.

It must have rained during the night. In the morning there was nothing on the other side of the fence but mud.

———————

THE NONEXISTENCE OF RUTABAGAS

I t has taken me some time to determine this, but I have been forced to come to the conclusion that rutabagas are not real. The rutabaga is a mythological vegetable.

Do you know anyone who has ever eaten a rutabaga? Has even one of your friends ever purchased a rutabaga? Of course not, because rutabagas are not real.

Go into the supermarket and stroll through the produce section. Hum along with the Muzak and see if you can find the rutabagas. Ask the nice young man stacking carrots where the rutabagas are. He will look at you and shake his head gently, for there are no rutabagas in the supermarket. There are no rutabagas in the supermarket because rutabagas do not exist. If they did, your supermarket certainly would sell them.

Some folks will tell you that you can buy rutabagas at the West Side Market. Do not believe them. They are the same people who will try to tell you that kohlrabi is real. The West Side Market isn't real, either. If it were, it certainly would have Muzak.

My dictionary defines rutabaga as a plant with an edible root that tastes like a turnip. An edible root that tastes like a turnip . . . isn't that an inherent contradiction? Of course, I don't believe it because I know rutabagas are not real, although turnips, regrettably, are. It does explain why no one would consider eating a rutabaga if it were real.

That venerable volume, *The Joy of Cooking*, gives only one recipe for rutabagas. Only one, mind you, in a book that details 34 different ways to cook potatoes and 13 ways to serve eggplant. Ah hah, you say! Why would *The Joy of Cooking* give any recipe, even one, for a mythological vegetable? Would *The Joy of Cooking* tell you how to cook something if it weren't real? Would it?

Well, why not? No doubt the rutabaga recipe was included merely to provide a sort of culinary comic relief . . . a pleasant note of whimsy in an otherwise pedestrian work. Besides, would you believe a book that also contains a recipe for kohlrabi?

DON'T LOAN THIS BOOK TO YOUR FRIENDS!

Let them buy their own copies.

Better still, buy the book for them.
They'll love you for it.

The Nonexistence of Rutabagas and Other Marginal Considerations is the perfect gift for Christmas, Mother's Day, Beethoven's Birthday, Halloween, Groundhog's Day, the Fourth of July or your best friend's anniversary. One size fits all!